PRAISE FOR #1 *NEW YORK TIMES* BESTSELLING AUTHOR SANDRA BROWN

"[Brown] is a masterful storyteller, carefully crafting tales that keep readers on the edge of their seats."
—*USA Today*

"Author Sandra Brown proves herself top-notch."
—Associated Press

"Sandra Brown has continued to grow with every novel."
—*Dallas Morning News*

"Brown's storytelling gift is surprisingly rare, even among crowd-pleasers."
—*Toronto Sun*

"A novelist who can't write them fast enough."
—*San Antonio Express-News*

"Brown has few to envy among living authors."
—*Kirkus Reviews*

"A taut, seamless tale of nonstop action...A revel not to be missed."
—*BookPage*

"Sandra Brown is a master at weaving a story of suspense into a tight web that catches and holds the reader from the first page to the last."
—*Library Journal*

STANDOFF

STANDOFF

SANDRA BROWN

GRAND CENTRAL
PUBLISHING

NEW YORK BOSTON

Grand Central Publishing
Hachette Book Group
1290 Avenue of the Americas, New York, NY 10104
grandcentralpublishing.com
twitter.com/grandcentralpub

Originally published in hardcover by Grand Central Publishing in May 2000
This trade paperback edition published in July 2017

Grand Central Publishing is a division of Hachette Book Group, Inc. The Grand Central Publishing name and logo is a trademark of Hachette Book Group, Inc.

The publisher is not responsible for websites (or their content) that are not owned by the publisher.

The Hachette Speakers Bureau provides a wide range of authors for speaking events. To find out more, go to www.hachettespeakersbureau.com or call (866) 376-6591.

Library of Congress Control Number: 99052374

ISBN: 978-1-5387-4477-2

Printed in the United States of America

LSC-C

10 9 8 7 6 5 4 3 2 1

STANDOFF

Chapter 1

I just heard the news bulletin on my car radio."

Tiel McCoy didn't begin this telephone conversation with any superfluous chitchat. That was her opening statement the instant Gully said hello. No preamble was necessary. Truth be known, he had probably been expecting her call.

But he played dumb anyway. "That you, Tiel? Enjoying your vacation so far?"

Her vacation had officially begun that morning when she left Dallas and headed west on Interstate 20. She had driven as far as Abilene, where she stopped to visit her uncle, who'd lived in a nursing home there for the past five years. She remembered Uncle Pete as a tall, robust man with an irreverent sense of humor, who could barbecue a mean brisket and knock a softball out of the park.

Today they had shared a lunch of soggy fish sticks and canned English peas and watched an episode of *Guiding Light*. She'd asked if there was anything she could do for him while she was there, like write a letter or buy a magazine. He had smiled at her sadly and thanked her for coming, then gave himself over to an attendant who'd tucked him in for his nap like a child.

Outside the nursing home, Tiel had gratefully inhaled the scorching, gritty West Texas air in the hope of eradicating the smell of age and resignation which had permeated the facility. She had been relieved the family obligation was behind her, but felt guilty for the relief. By an act of will she shook off her despair and reminded herself that she was on vacation.

It wasn't even officially summer yet, but it was unseasonably warm for May. There'd been no shade in which to park at the nursing home; consequently her car's interior had been so hot she could have baked cookies on the dashboard. She flipped on the AC full-blast and found a radio station that played something other than Garth, George, and Willie.

"I'm going to have a wonderful time. The time away will be good for me. I'll feel a lot better for having done it." She repeated this internal dialogue like a catechism, trying to convince herself of the truth of it. She had approached the vacation as though it were equivalent to taking a bad-tasting laxative.

Heat waves made the highway appear to ripple, and the undulating movement was hypnotic. The driving became mindless. Her mind drifted. The radio provided background noise of which Tiel was barely aware.

But hearing the news bulletin was like getting goosed by the driver's seat. With a lurch, everything accelerated— the car, Tiel's heart rate, her mind.

Immediately she fished her cell phone from her large leather satchel and placed the call to Gully's direct line. Again declining any unnecessary conversation, she said to him now, "Give me the skinny."

"What's the radio putting out?"

"That earlier today a high school student in Fort Worth kidnaped Russell Dendy's daughter."

"That's about the gist of it," Gully confirmed.

"The gist, but I want details."

"You're on vacation, Tiel."

"I'm coming back. Next exit, I'll make a U-turn." She consulted her dashboard clock. "I'll be at the station by—"

"Hold on, hold on. Where're you at, exactly?"

"About fifty miles west of Abilene."

"Hmm."

"What, Gully?" Her palms had become damp. She experienced the familiar tickle in her belly that only happened when she was following a hot lead to a super story. That unique adrenaline rush couldn't be mistaken.

"You're on your way to Angel Fire, right?"

"Right."

"Northeastern part of New Mexico...Yeah, there it is." He must have been reading a highway map as he spoke. "Naw, never mind. You don't want this assignment, Tiel. It would take you out of your way."

He was baiting her, and she knew he was baiting her, but in this instance she didn't mind being baited. She wanted a piece of this story. The kidnaping of Russell Dendy's daughter was big news, and it promised to become even bigger news before it was over. "I don't mind taking a detour. Tell me where to go."

"Well," he hedged, "only if you're sure."

"I'm sure."

"Okay then. Not too far in front of you is a turnoff onto state highway Two-oh-eight. Take it south to San Angelo. On the south side of San Angelo you're gonna intersect with—"

"Gully, about how far out of my way is this detour going to take me?"

"I thought you didn't care."

"I don't. I'd just like to know. Rough estimate."

"Well, let's see. Give or take...about three hundred miles."

"From Angel Fire?" she asked faintly.

"From where you are now. Doesn't count the rest of the way to Angel Fire."

"Three hundred round trip?"

"One way."

She expelled a long sigh, but was careful not to let him hear it. "You said highway Two-oh-eight south to San Angelo, then what?"

She steered with her knee, held the phone with her left hand, and took notes with her right. The car was on cruise control, but her brain was in overdrive. Journalistic juices were pumping faster than the pistons in her engine. Thoughts of long pleasant evenings spent in a porch rocker were swapped for those of sound bites and interviews.

But she was getting ahead of herself. She lacked pertinent facts. When she asked for them, Gully, damn him, turned mulish on her. "Not now, Tiel. I'm as busy as a one-armed paperhanger, and you've got miles to cover. By the time you get where you're going, I'll have a lot more info."

Frustrated and supremely irked with him for being so stingy with the details, she asked, "What's the name of the town again?"

"Hera."

The highways were arrow-straight, flanked on both sides by endless prairie with only an occasional herd of cattle grazing in irrigated pastures. Oil wells were silhouetted against a cloudless horizon. Frequently a tumbleweed rolled across the roadway in front of her. Once she got beyond San Angelo, she rarely saw another vehicle.

Funny, she thought, *the way things turn out.*

Ordinarily she would have elected to fly to New Mexico. But days ago she had decided to drive to Angel Fire, not only so she could visit Uncle Pete along the way, but also to get herself into a holiday frame of mind. The long drive would give her time to decompress, work the kinks out, begin the period of rest and relaxation before she ever reached the mountain resort, so that when she did arrive, she would already be in vacation mode.

At home in Dallas, she moved with the speed of light, always in a rush, always working under a deadline. This morning, once she had reached the western fringe of Fort Worth and put the metropolitan sprawl behind her, when the vacation became a reality, she had begun to anticipate the idyllic days awaiting her. She had daydreamed of clear, gurgling streams, hikes along trails lined with aspens, cool, crisp air, and lazy mornings spent with a cup of coffee and a fiction best-seller.

There would be no schedule to keep, nothing but hours in which to be lazy, which was a virtue unto itself. Tiel McCoy was way past due to engage in some unabashed ennui. She'd already postponed this vacation three times.

"Use 'em or lose 'em," Gully had told her of the vacation days she had accumulated.

He had lectured her on how her performance, as well as her disposition, would greatly improve if she gave herself a breather. This from the man who hadn't taken more than a few vacation days in the past forty-something years—counting the week required to have his gallbladder removed.

When she reminded him of this, he had scowled at her. "Precisely. You want to wind up an ugly, shriveled, pathetic relic like me?" Then he'd really hit the nail on the head. "Taking a vacation isn't going to jeopardize your chances. That job'll still be up for grabs when you get back."

She easily inferred the meaning behind that sly remark. Miffed at him for homing in on the real reason behind her reluctance to leave work for any period of time, she had grudgingly consented to going away for a week. The reservations had been made, the trip scheduled. But every schedule should have a little bit of flexibility built in.

And if flexibility was ever called for, it was when Russell Dendy's daughter was allegedly kidnaped.

Tiel held the pay phone's sticky receiver pinched between the pads of her thumb and index finger, loathe to touch any more of the surface than necessary. "Okay, Gully, I'm here. Well, near, at least. Actually, I'm lost."

He cackled. "Too excited to concentrate on where you're going?"

"Well, it's not like I've missed a thriving metropolis. You said yourself, the place isn't even on most maps."

Her sense of humor had worn off about the time she'd lost all feeling in her butt. Hours ago, her posterior had gone numb from sitting. Since talking to him, she had stopped only once, and then only out of extreme necessity. She was hungry, thirsty, tired, cranky, achy, and none too fresh because she'd been facing into the setting sun for a long portion of the trip. The car's AC had gone humid from overuse. A shower would be bliss.

Gully didn't improve her mood any by asking, "How'd you manage to get lost?"

"I lost my sense of direction after the sun went down. The landscape looks the same from every angle out here. Even more so after dark. I'm calling from a convenience store in a town with a population of eight hundred twenty-three, according to the city-limit sign, and I think the chamber of commerce fudged that number in their favor. This is the only lighted building for miles around. The town is called Rojo something."

"Flats. Rojo Flats."

Naturally Gully knew the full name of this obscure hamlet. He probably knew the mayor's name. Gully knew everything. He was a walking encyclopedia. He collected information the way frat rats collected coeds' phone numbers.

The TV station where Tiel worked had a news director, but the man with the title conducted business from inside a carpeted office and was more a bean counter and administrator than a hands-on boss.

The man in the trenches, the one who dealt directly with the reporters, writers, photographers, and editors, the one who coordinated schedules and listened to sob stories and chewed ass when ass-chewing was called for, the one who actually ran the news operation, was the assignments editor, Gully.

He'd been at the station when it signed on in the early fifties, and had mandated that they would have to carry him out of the place feetfirst. He would die before he retired. He worked a sixteen-hour day and begrudged the time he wasn't working. He had a colorful vocabulary and countless similes, an extensive repertoire of yarns about bygone days in broadcast news, and seemingly no life beyond the newsroom. His first name was Yarborough, but only a few living persons knew that. Everyone else knew him strictly as Gully.

"Are you going to give me this mysterious assignment or not?"

He wouldn't be rushed. "What happened to your vacation plans?"

"Nothing. I'm still on vacation."

"Uh-huh."

"I am! I'm not canceling my week off. I'm just postponing the start of it, that's all."

"What's the new boyfriend gonna say?"

"I've told you a thousand times, there is no new boyfriend." He laughed his phlegmy, chain-smoker's laugh that said he knew she was lying, and that she knew he knew.

"Got your notepad?" he asked suddenly.

"Uh, yeah."

Whatever germs had been teeming on the telephone were probably living with her now. Reconciled to that, she propped the receiver on her shoulder and held it there with her cheek while she removed a notepad and pen from her satchel and placed them on the narrow metal ledge beneath the wall-mounted telephone.

"Shoot."

"The boy's name is Ronald Davison," Gully began.

"I heard that much on the radio."

"Goes by Ronnie. Senior year, same as the Dendy girl. Won't graduate with any honors, but he's a solid B student. Never in trouble until today. After homeroom this morning, he boogied out of the student parking lot in his Toyota pickup with Sabra Dendy riding shotgun."

"Russ Dendy's child."

"His one and only."

"Is the FBI on it?"

"FBI. Texas Rangers. You name it. If it wears a badge, it's working this one. Waco all over again. Everybody's claiming jurisdiction and wants in on the action."

Tiel took a moment to absorb the broad scope of this story. The short hallway in which the pay phone was located led to the public rest rooms. One had a cowgirl in a fringed skirt stenciled in blue paint on the door. The other, predictably, had a similar silhouette of a cowpoke in chaps and ten-gallon hat, twirling a lasso above his head.

Glancing down the hall, Tiel spotted the real thing coming into the store. Tall, slender, Stetson pulled down low on his forehead. He nodded toward the store's cashier, whose frizzy, overpermed hair had been dyed an unflattering shade of ocher.

Nearer to Tiel was an elderly couple browsing for souvenirs, apparently in no hurry to return to their Winnebago. At least Tiel assumed the Winnebago at the gas pumps outside belonged to them. Through bifocal eyeglasses the lady was reading the ingredients of a jar on the shelf. Tiel heard her exclaim, "Jalapeño pepper *jelly*? Good Lord."

The couple then joined Tiel in the hallway, moving toward their respective rest rooms. "Don't dally, Gladys," the man said. His white legs were virtually hairless and looked ridiculously thin in his baggy khaki shorts and thick-soled athletic shoes.

"You mind your business, and I'll mind mine," she retorted smartly. As she moved past Tiel she gave her a men-think-they're-so-smart-but-we-know-better wink. Another time, Tiel would have thought the senior couple cute and endearing. But she was thoughtfully reading what she'd taken down almost verbatim from Gully.

"You said 'riding shotgun.' Strange choice of words, Gully."

"Can you keep a secret?" He lowered his voice significantly. "Because my ass will be grass if this gets out before our next newscast. We've scooped every other station and newspaper in the state."

Tiel's scalp began to tingle, as it did when she knew she was hearing something that no other reporter had heard, when she had uncovered the element that would set her story apart from all the others, when her exclusive had the potential of winning her a journalism prize or praise from her peers. Or of guaranteeing her the coveted spot on *Nine Live.*

"Who would I tell, Gully? I'm sharing space with a fresh-off-the-range cowboy buying a six-pack of Bud, a sassy granny lady and her husband from out of state—I'm guessing by their accents. And two non-English-speaking Mexicans." The pair had since come into the store. She'd overheard them speaking Spanish while heating packaged burritos in a microwave oven.

Gully said, "Linda—"

"Linda? She got the story?"

"You're on vacation, remember?"

"A vacation you urged me to take!" Tiel exclaimed.

Linda Harper was another reporter, a darned good reporter, and Tiel's unspoken rival. It stung that Gully had assigned Linda to cover such a plum of a story, which rightfully should have belonged to her. At least that's the way she saw it.

"You want to hear this or not?" he asked cantankerously.

"Go ahead."

The elderly man emerged from the men's room. He moved to the end of the hall, where he paused to wait for his wife. To kill time, he took a camcorder from a nylon airline bag and began tinkering with it.

Gully said, "Linda interviewed Sabra Dendy's best friend this afternoon. Hold on to your hat. The Dendy girl is pregnant with Ronnie Davison's kid. Eight months gone. They've been hiding it."

"You're kidding! And the Dendys didn't know?"

"According to the friend, nobody did. That is, not until last night. The kids broke the news to their parents, and Russ Dendy went apeshit."

Tiel's mind was already racing ahead, filling in the blanks. "So this isn't a kidnaping. It's a contemporary Romeo and Juliet."

"I didn't say that."

"But...?"

"But that'd be my first guess. A view shared by Sabra Dendy's best friend and confidante. She claims Ronnie Davison is crazy about Sabra and wouldn't harm a hair on her head. Said Russell Dendy has been fighting this romance for more than a year. Nobody's good enough for his daughter, they're too young to know their own minds, college is a must, and so forth. You get the picture."

"I do."

And what was wrong with the picture was that Tiel McCoy wasn't in it and Linda Harper was. Damn! Of all times to go on vacation.

"I'm coming back tonight, Gully."

"No."

"I think you sent me on this wild goose chase so it would be impossible for me to return."

"Not true."

"How far am I from El Paso?"

"El Paso? Who said anything about El Paso?"

"Or San Antonio. Whichever is closer. I could drive there tonight and hop a Southwest flight in the morning. Do you have their schedule handy? What time does the first flight depart for Dallas?"

"Listen to me, Tiel. We've got it covered. Bob's working the manhunt–law enforcement angle. Linda's on the kids' friends, teachers, and families. Steve's practically moved into the Dendys' mansion, so he'll be there if a ransom call comes in, which I don't expect. And, bottom line, those kids'll probably turn up before you could get back to Dallas anyway."

"So what am I doing out here in the middle of freaking nowhere?"

The old man shot her a curious glance over his shoulder.

"Listen," Gully hissed. "The friend? Sabra mentioned to her a few weeks back that she and Ronnie might just hightail it to Mexico."

Mollified because she was closer to the Mexican border than she was to Dallas, Tiel asked, "Where in Mexico?"

"She didn't know. Or wouldn't say. Linda had to twist her arm to get that much from her. She didn't want to betray Sabra's confidence. But the one thing she did say is that Ronnie's dad—his real dad; his mom's remarried—is sympathetic to their predicament. A while back he offered his help if they ever needed it. Now, you're gonna feel really bad about yelling at me when I tell you where he hangs his hat."

"Hera."

"Satisfied?"

She should have apologized, but she didn't. Gully understood. "Who else knows about this?"

"Nobody. But they will. It works to our advantage that Hera is a one-horse town, not on any beaten path."

"Tell me about it," she muttered.

"When word gets out, it'll take everybody a while to get there, even by helicopter. You've got a definite head start."

"Gully, I love you!" she said excitedly. "Direct me out of here."

The elderly lady emerged from the ladies' room and rejoined her husband. She admonished him for fiddling with the camcorder and ordered him to put it back in the tote bag before he broke it.

"Like you're an expert with video cameras," the old man retorted.

"I took the time to read the instruction book. You didn't."

Tiel poked her finger in her ear so she could hear Gully better. "What's the dad's name? Davison, I presume."

"I've got an address and phone number."

Tiel wrote down the information as fast as he reeled it off. "Do I have an appointment with him?"

"Working on it. He might not agree to go on camera."

"I'll get him to agree," she said confidently.

"I'm dispatching a chopper with a photographer."

"Kip if he's available."

"Y'all can meet in Hera. You'll do the interview tomorrow as soon as it's arranged with Davison. Then you can continue on your merry way."

"Unless there's more story there."

"Uh-uh. That's the condition, Tiel." She envisioned him stubbornly shaking his head. "You do this bit, then you're off to Angel Fire. Period. End of discussion."

"Whatever you say." She could easily agree now, then argue about it later if events warranted.

"Okay, let's see. Outta Rojo Flats…" The map must have been right there on his desk, because within seconds he was giving her further directions. "Shouldn't take you long to get there. You're not sleepy, are you?"

She was never more wide awake than when pursuing a story. Her problem was shutting her mind off and going to sleep. "I'll buy something caffeinated to take along."

"Check in with me as soon as you get there. I've got you a room reserved at the only motel. You can't miss it. I'm told it's at the blinking traffic light—the one and only. They'll wait up for you to give you a room key." Changing subjects, he asked, "Is the new boyfriend going to be pissed?"

"For the last time, Gully, there is no new boyfriend."

She hung up and placed another call—to her new boyfriend.

Joseph Marcus was as much a workaholic as she was. He was scheduled to fly out early the next day, so she predicted he would be working late at his desk, putting things in order prior to his being away for several days. She was right. He answered his office phone on the second ring.

"Do you get paid overtime?" she teased.

"Tiel? Hi. I'm glad you called."

"It's after hours. I was afraid you wouldn't answer."

"Reflex. Where are you?"

"The end of nowhere."

"Everything okay? You haven't had car trouble or anything?"

"No, everything's great. I called for a couple of reasons. First, because I miss you."

This was the tack to take. Establish that the trip was still on. Establish that it was being delayed, not derailed. Assure him that everything was cool, then inform him of the slight wrinkle in their plans for a romantic getaway.

"You saw me just last night."

"But only briefly, and it's been a long day. Secondly, I called to remind you to throw a swimsuit into your suitcase. The hot tub at the condo complex is public."

After a pause, he said, "Actually, Tiel, it's good that you called. I needed to talk to you."

Something in the tone of his voice prevented her from prattling on. She stopped talking and waited for him to fill the silence that yawned between them.

"I could have called you on your cell phone today, but this isn't the sort of thing... The fact is... And I'm sorry as hell about this. You can't begin to know how sorry I am."

Tiel stared at the countless perforations in the metal surrounding the telephone. She stared so long without blinking that the tiny holes ran together. Absently she wondered what purpose they served.

"I'm afraid I can't get away tomorrow."

She'd been holding her breath. Now she released it, relieved. His change of plans alleviated her guilt over having to change them herself.

However, before she could speak, he continued. "I know how much you'd looked forward to this trip. And so had I," he rushed to add.

"Let me make this easier on you, Joseph." Meekly she confessed. "The truth is, I was calling to say that I need another couple days before I can get to Angel Fire. So I'm fine with a short postponement. Would your schedule allow us to meet on, say, Tuesday instead of to-morrow?"

"You don't understand what I'm saying, Tiel. I can't meet you at all."

The perforations ran together again. "Oh. I see. That is disappointing. Well—"

"It's been very tense around here. My wife found my airline ticket and—"

"Excuse me?"

"I said my wife found—"

"You're married?"

"Well...yeah. I thought you knew."

"No." Her facial muscles felt stiff and inflexible. "You have failed to mention a Mrs. Marcus."

"Because my marriage has nothing to do with you, with us. It hasn't been a *real* marriage for a long time. Once I've explained my situation at home to you, you'll understand."

"You're married." This time it was a statement, not a question.

"Tiel, listen—"

"No, no, I'm not going to listen, Joseph. What I'm going to do is hang up on you, you son of a bitch."

The telephone receiver she had been so reluctant even to touch ten minutes earlier she now clung to long after replacing it on the hook. She leaned against the pay phone, her forehead pressing hard against the per-forated metal while her hands maintained their grip on the greasy receiver.

Married. He had seemed too good to be true, and he was. Good-looking, charming, friendly, witty, ath-letic, successful, and financially secure Joseph Marcus was married. If not for an airline ticket she would have had an affair with a married man.

She swallowed a surge of nausea and took another moment to compose herself. Later she would lick her wounded ego, berate herself for being such a Pollyanna, and curse him to hell and back. But right now she had work to do.

Joseph's revelation had left her reeling with disbelief. She was furious beyond measure. She was terribly hurt, but more than anything she was embarrassed by her gullibility. All the more reason she was not about to let the bastard affect her work performance.

Work was her panacea, her life support. When she was happy, she worked. Sad, she worked. Sick, she worked. Work was the cure for all her ills. Work was the remedy for everything...even heartbreak so profound you thought you'd die.

She knew that firsthand.

She gathered up her pride, along with her notes on the Dendy story and Gully's directions to Hera, Texas, and ordered herself to mobilize.

Compared to the dimness of the hallway, the fluorescent lighting in the store seemed inordinately bright. The cowboy had left. The elderly couple were browsing through the array of magazines. The two Spanish-speaking men were eating their burritos and talking quietly together.

Tiel sensed their smoldering gazes as she went past them on her way to the refrigerated cabinets. One said something to the other that caused him to snicker. It was easy to guess the nature of the comment. Thankfully, her Spanish was rusty.

She slid open the door to the refrigerator and selected a six-pack of high-voltage cola for the road. From a rack of snack food she chose a package of sunflower seeds. During college she had discovered that cracking open the salty seeds in order to get to the kernel inside was a good manual exercise to keep one awake while studying. Hopefully it would translate to night driving as well.

She debated whether or not to buy a bag of chocolate-covered caramels. Just because a man she had been dating for weeks had turned out to be a married shit-heel didn't mean she should use that as an excuse to binge. On the other hand, if ever she deserved a treat—

The security camera in the corner of the ceiling virtually exploded, sending pieces of glass and metal flying.

Instinctively Tiel recoiled from the deafening noise. But the camera hadn't exploded on its own. A young man had entered the store and fired a pistol at it. The gunman then aimed his weapon at the cashier, who screeched a high note before the sound seemed to freeze inside her throat.

"This is a holdup," he said melodramatically, and somewhat needlessly, since it was apparent what it was.

To the young woman who had accompanied him into the store, he said, "Sabra, watch the others. If anyone moves, warn me."

"Okay, Ronnie."

Well, I might die, Tiel thought. *But at least I'll get my story.*

And she wouldn't be going to Hera to get it. It had come to her.

Chapter 2

Y ou!" Ronnie Davison pointed the pistol at Tiel. "Come over here. Lie down on the floor." Incapable of moving, she only gaped at him. "Now!"

Dropping her package of sunflower seeds and the six-pack of sodas, she scrambled over to the indicated spot and lay facedown as instructed. Now that her initial shock had worn off, she bit her tongue to keep from asking him why he was compounding a kidnaping with an armed robbery.

But she doubted that at this moment the young man would be receptive to questions. Besides, until she knew what he had planned for her and the other eyewitnesses, perhaps she shouldn't reveal that she was a reporter and knew his and his accomplice's identities.

"Get over here and lie down," he ordered the elderly couple. "You two." He pointed the gun at the Mexican men. "Now! Move it!"

The old people complied without argument. The

Mexican men remained where they were. "I'll shoot you if you don't get over here!" Ronnie shouted.

Keeping her head down and addressing her words to the floor, Tiel said, "They don't speak English."

"Shut up!"

Ronnie Davison broke the language barrier and made himself understood by motioning with the pistol. Moving slowly, reluctantly, the men joined Tiel and the elderly couple on the floor.

"Put your hands behind your head."

Tiel and the others did as he asked.

Over the years, Tiel had covered dozens of news stories wherein innocent bystanders, who had become eyewitnesses to a crime, were all too often found at the scene, lying facedown, dead, one gunshot to the back of the head, executed for no other reason except that they had been in the wrong place at the wrong time. Was this to be how her life ended?

Strangely, she wasn't so much afraid as angry. She hadn't done everything she wanted to do! Snowboarding looked like a real kick, but she hadn't had time to try it. Correction: She hadn't *taken* time to try it. She'd never toured the Napa Valley. She wanted to see Paris again, not as a high school student under strict supervision, but on her own, free to meander the boulevards at will.

There were goals she had yet to reach. Think of the stories she would miss covering if her life ended now. *Nine Live* would go to Linda Harper by default, and that was so unfair.

And not all her dreams were career-oriented. She and other single friends joked about their biological clocks, but in private she anguished over its incessant tick. If she died tonight, having a child would be just one of many dreams left unfulfilled.

Then there was the other thing. The big thing. The powerful guilt that fueled her ambition. She hadn't done enough yet to make up for that. She hadn't yet atoned for harsh words spoken angrily and flippantly, which, tragically, had been prophetic. She must live to make restitution for that.

She held her breath, waiting for death.

But Davison's attention was on something else. "You, in the corner," the young man shouted. "Now! Or I'll kill the old folks. It's up to you."

Tiel raised her head only high enough to glance into the fish-eye mirror mounted in the corner at the ceiling. Her assumption had been wrong. The cowboy hadn't left. In the mirror, she watched him calmly replace a paperback novel in its slot on the revolving rack. As he sauntered down the aisle, he removed his hat and set it on top of a shelf. Tiel experienced a flurry of recognition, but she attributed it to having seen him before when he came into the store.

The eyes he kept trained on Ronnie Davison had a tracery of fine lines at the corners. Unsmiling lips. The face said *Don't mess with me*, and Ronnie Davison read it well. Nervously he shifted the pistol from one hand to the other until the cowboy was stretched out alongside one of the Mexican men, his hands clasped on the back of his head.

While all this was going on, the cashier had been emptying the cash drawer into a plastic grocery bag. Apparently this out-of-the-way store wasn't equipped with an after-dark safe into which cash automatically went. From what Tiel could discern, there was an appreciable amount of money in the sack Sabra Dendy took from the cashier.

"I've got the money, Ronnie," said the daughter of one of Fort Worth's richest men.

"Okay then." He hesitated as though unsure about what to do next. "You," he said, addressing the terrified cashier. "Lie down with the rest of them."

She might have weighed ninety pounds sopping wet and was a stranger to sunscreen. The skin hanging loosely from her bony arms looked like leather, Tiel noticed as the tiny woman lay down beside her. Little hiccups of terror erupted from her spasmodically.

. Everyone had his own unique way of reacting to fear. The elderly couple had disobeyed Ronnie's orders to keep both hands behind their heads. The man's right hand was tightly clasping his wife's left.

This is it, Tiel thought. *He'll kill us now.*

She closed her eyes and tried to pray, but it had been a while and she was out of practice. The poetic language of the King James Bible eluded her. She wanted this appeal to be eloquent and stirring, persuasive and impressive, compelling enough to distract God from all the other prayers coming His way at this particular moment.

But God probably wouldn't approve of her purely selfish reasons for wanting to live anyhow, so all she could think to say was, "Heavenly Father, please don't let me die."

When the scream rent the silence, Tiel thought for certain it had originated from the cashier. She glanced quickly at the woman beside her, to see what unspeakable torture had been inflicted. But the woman was still blubbering, not screaming.

It was Sabra Dendy who had screamed, and that first startling sound was followed by, "Oh, my God! *Ronnie!*"

The boy rushed over to her. "Sabra? What's the matter? What's happening?"

"I think it's...Oh, Lord."

Tiel couldn't help herself. She raised her head to see what was going on. The girl was whimpering and staring aghast at the puddle of fluid between her feet.

"Her water broke."

Ronnie whipped his head around and glared at Tiel. "What?"

"Her water broke." She repeated the statement with more composure than she felt. Actually her heart was hammering. This might be the spark that set him off and caused him to bring things to a swift conclusion, such as shooting them all and then dealing with his girlfriend's crisis.

"That's right, young man." Unafraid, the elderly woman sat up and addressed him with the temerity she had demonstrated when lecturing her husband about fiddling with the home video camera. "Her baby's coming."

"Ronnie? Ronnie?" Sabra crammed the skirt of her sundress up between her thighs, as though to impede the course of nature. On bended knees, she lowered herself to the floor until she was sitting back on her heels. "What are we going to do?"

Clearly the girl was frightened. Neither she nor Ronnie seemed adept at armed robbery. Or at childbirth, for that matter. Taking courage from the older lady, Tiel also sat up. "I suggest—"

"You shut up," Ronnie shouted. "Everybody just shut up!"

He kept his pistol aimed at them as he knelt down beside Sabra. "Are they right? This means the baby's coming?"

"I think so." She nodded, shaking loose tears and sending them rolling down her cheeks. "I'm sorry."

"It's okay. How much time... How long before it's born?"

"I don't know. It varies, I think."

"Does it hurt?"

A fresh batch of tears formed in her eyes. "It's been hurting for a couple of hours."

"A couple of hours!" he cried in alarm.

"But only a little. Not bad."

"How long since it started? Why didn't you tell me?"

"If she's been in labor—"

"I told you to shut up!" he yelled at Tiel.

"If she's been in labor for a while," she said persistently, keeping her eyes steadfastly on his, "you'd better get medical attention. Immediately."

"No," Sabra said hastily. "Don't listen to her, Ronnie." She grabbed his sleeve. "I'm okay. I'm—"

A pain seized her. Her face contorted. She gasped for breath.

"Oh, God. Oh, Jesus." Ronnie studied Sabra's face, raking his teeth across his lower lip. His gun hand wavered.

One of the Mexican men—the shorter of the two—surged to his feet and lunged toward the couple.

"No!" Tiel shouted.

The cowboy made a grab for the Mexican's leg, but missed.

Ronnie fired the pistol.

The bullet shattered the glass door of the refrigerated compartment, making a horrific sound and puncturing a plastic gallon jug. Everything nearby was showered with glass and milk.

The Mexican man drew up short. Before he came to a complete rest, inertia caused his body to rock slightly forward, then back, as though his boots had become stuck to the floor.

"Stay back or I'll shoot you!" Ronnie's face was congested with blood. A common language wasn't required to get his message across. The man's taller friend spoke to him softly and urgently in Spanish. He backed away until he reached his starting point, then sat down again.

Tiel glared at him. "You could have gotten your fool head blown off. Save your machismo for another time, okay? I don't want to get killed because of it."

Although the words were unknown to him, he caught her drift. Pridefully, his dark eyes smoldered resentment over being dressed down by a woman, but she didn't care.

Tiel turned back to the young couple. Sabra was now lying on her side, her knees drawn up to her chest. For the moment she was quiet.

By contrast, Ronnie looked on the verge of losing all self-control. Tiel didn't believe that, in the span of a single afternoon, he could have been transformed from a student who'd never been in trouble into a cold-blooded killer. She didn't think the boy had it in him to kill anyone, even in self-defense. If he had wanted to hit the man who had charged him, he could have easily. Instead he appeared as upset as anyone that he'd had to fire the pistol. Tiel guessed that he had intentionally missed the man and fired the gun only to underscore his threat.

Or she could be entirely, terribly wrong.

According to Gully's information, Ronnie Davison came from a broken home. His real father lived far away, so visits couldn't have been too frequent. Ronnie lived with his mother and stepfather. What if little Ronnie had had a problem with those arrangements? What if his personality had been twisted by the forced separation from his father, and for years he'd been harboring hatred and mistrust? What if he had been concealing murderous impulses as successfully as he and Sabra had concealed her pregnancy? What if he'd been driven over the edge by Russell Dendy's reaction to their news? He was desperate, and desperation was a dangerous motivator.

For speaking out, she would probably be the first one he shot. But she couldn't just lie there and die without at least trying to avoid it. "If you care anything for this girl…"

"I've told you before to shut up."

"I'm only trying to prevent a disaster, Ronnie." Since he and Sabra had addressed each other, he wouldn't wonder how she knew his name. "If you don't get help for Sabra, you're going to regret it for the rest of your life." He was listening, so she took advantage of his apparent indecision. "I assume the child is yours."

"What the hell do you think? Of course it's mine."

"Then I'm sure you're concerned for its well-being as much as you are for Sabra's. She needs medical assistance."

"Don't listen to her, Ronnie," Sabra said weakly. "The pain's better now. Maybe it's a false alarm, after all. I'll be okay if I can just rest for a while."

"I could take you to a hospital. There's got to be one fairly close."

"No!" Sabra sat up and gripped his shoulders. "He'd find out. He'd come after us. No. We're driving straight through to Mexico tonight. Now that we've got some money, we can make it."

"I could call my dad…."

She shook her head. "Daddy could've got to him by now. Bribed him or something. We're on our own, Ronnie, and that's how I want it. Help me up. Let's get out of here." But as she struggled to get up, another pain seized her and she gripped her distended abdomen. "Oh my God, oh my God."

"This is nuts." Before Tiel had time to process the command of her brain, she was on her feet.

"Hey!" Ronnie shouted. "Get back down."

Tiel ignored him, moved past him, and crouched down beside the suffering girl. "Sabra?" She took her hand. "Squeeze my hand until the pain passes. That might help."

Sabra grasped her hand so hard Tiel feared the bones would be ground to meal. But she endured it, and together they rode out the contraction. When the girl's features began to relax, Tiel whispered, "Better now?"

"Hmm." Then with a trace of panic, "Where's Ronnie?"

"He's right here."

"I won't leave you, Sabra."

Tiel said, "I think you should urge him to call nine-one-one for you."

"No."

"But you're at risk and so is your baby."

"He would find us. He'd catch us."

"Who?" Tiel asked, although she knew. Russell Dendy. He had the reputation of being a ruthless businessman. From what she knew of him, Tiel couldn't imagine him being any less unyielding in his personal relationships.

Ronnie said brusquely, "Get back with the others, lady. This is none of your business."

"You made it my business when you waved a pistol at me and threatened my life."

"Get back over there."

"No."

"Look, lady…"

He faltered when a car pulled off the highway and into the parking lot. Its headlights swept the front of the store.

"Damn! Hey, lady!" He walked over to the cashier and nudged her with the toe of his shoe. "Get up. Turn off the lights and lock the door."

The woman shook her head, refusing to acknowledge either him or the precarious situation.

"Do what he says," the elderly woman said to her. "We'll be all right if we just do what he says."

"Hurry up!" The car rolled to a stop at one of the gas pumps. "Turn off the lights and lock the door."

The woman came to her feet unsteadily. "I'm not supposed to close until eleven. That's still ten minutes."

If circumstances hadn't been so tense, Tiel would have laughed at her blind adherence to the rules.

Ronnie said, "Do it now. Before he gets out of his car."

She went behind the counter, her mules slapping against her heels. At the flip of a switch, the lights outside were extinguished.

"Now lock the door."

She click-clacked over to another control panel behind the counter and threw a switch. With an audible snap, the door locked electronically. "How do you unlock it?" Ronnie asked her.

He was smart, Tiel thought. He didn't want to get trapped inside.

"Just flip this here switch," the cashier replied.

The cowboy and the two Mexican men were still lying facedown on the floor, their hands on their heads. They couldn't be seen by the man approaching the door. Tiel and Sabra were also out of sight in the aisle between two rows of shelves.

"Everybody stay put." Ronnie duckwalked to the elderly lady and grabbed her arm, lifting her to her feet.

"No!" her husband cried. "Leave her alone."

"Shut up!" Ronnie ordered. "If anybody moves, I'm going to shoot her."

"He's not going to shoot me, Vern," she said to her husband. "I'll be all right, as long as everyone stays calm."

The woman followed Ronnie's instructions and crouched down with him behind a cylindrical cold-drink cooler. From above the rim, he had a clear view to the door.

The customer tested the door, discovered it locked, and called out. "Donna! You in there? How come you shut off the lights?"

Donna, cringing behind the counter, remained mute.

The customer peered through the glass. "There you are," he said, spotting her. "What gives?"

"Answer him," Ronnie instructed her in a whisper.

"I'm...s-sick," she said, loud enough to carry through the door.

"Hell, you ain't got nothing I ain't already had. Open up. All I need is ten dollars' worth o' gas and a six-pack o' Miller Lite."

"I cain't," she called out tearfully.

"Come on, Donna. Won't take two shakes, and I'll be on my way. It ain't quite 'leven yet. Open the door."

"I cain't." She unraveled at the same time her voice rose to a full-fledged scream. "He's gotta gun and he's gonna kill us all." She dropped down behind the counter.

"Shit!"

Tiel didn't know from which man the expletive had come, but it echoed exactly what she was thinking. She was also thinking that if Ronnie Davison didn't shoot Donna the cashier, she just might.

The man at the door backed away, then stumbled as he turned and ran for his car. Tires screeched as the vehicle shot backward, then spun around and pulled onto the highway.

The old man was chanting, "Don't hurt my wife. I beg you, please don't hurt Gladys. Don't hurt my Gladys."

"Hush, Vern. I'm all right."

Ronnie was angrily yelling at Donna for being so stupid. "Why'd you do that? Why? That guy will call the police. We'll be trapped here. Oh, hell, why'd you do that?"

His voice was tearing with frustration and fear. Tiel thought that he was probably as scared as the rest of them. Maybe more so. Because no matter how this situation was ultimately resolved, he would be faced not only with legal consequences, but with the wrath of Russell Dendy. God help him.

The young man ordered the cashier to come from behind the counter to where he could see her.

Tiel didn't know whether or not she obeyed him. All her attention was centered on the girl, who was in the grip of another contraction. "Squeeze my hand, Sabra. Breathe." Isn't that what women in labor were supposed to do? Breathe? That's what they did in the movies. They huffed and they puffed and...and they screamed the house down. "Breathe, Sabra."

"Hey! Hey!" Ronnie shouted suddenly. "Where do you think you're going? Get back over there and lie down. Hey, *I mean it!*"

Now wasn't the time to be provoking the rattled young man, and Tiel intended to tell whoever was doing

so to cut it out. She glanced up, but the reproach died
unspoken when the cowboy knelt down on the other
side of Sabra.

"Get away from her!" Ronnie jammed the barrel of
the pistol against the cowboy's temple, but it was ignored and so were the young man's shouted threats.

Hands that looked accustomed to handling tack and
fence posts were placed on the girl's abdomen. They
kneaded it gently.

"I can help her." His voice was scratchy, like he
hadn't spoken in a long time, like West Texas dust had
collected on his vocal cords. He looked up at Ronnie.
"They call me Doc."

"You're a doctor?" Tiel asked.

His calm gaze moved to her, and he repeated, "I can
help her."

Chapter 3

———◆———

You're not touching her," Ronnie said fiercely. "Take your lousy hands off her."

The man called Doc continued to press the girl's abdomen. "She's in either the first or second stage of labor. Without knowing how much she's dilated, it's hard to gauge how close she is to delivering. But her pains are coming frequently, so I'm guessing—"

"Guessing?"

Ignoring Ronnie, Doc patted Sabra's shoulder reassuringly. "Is this your first baby?"

"Yes, sir."

"You can call me Doc."

"Okay."

"How long since you first started noticing the pains?"

"At first I just felt funny, you know? Well, I guess you don't."

He smiled. "I have no personal experience of it, no. Describe to me how it felt."

"Like right before a period. Sort of."

"Pressure down there? And twinges like a bad case of cramps?"

"Yes. Real bad. And a backache. I thought I was just tired from riding in the pickup so long, but it got worse. I didn't want to say anything." Her eyes moved to Ronnie, who was hovering over Doc's broad shoulders. He was hanging on every word, but he kept the pistol trained on the people who were lined up like matchsticks on the floor.

"When did these symptoms start?" Doc asked.

"About three o'clock this afternoon."

"Jesus, Sabra," Ronnie groaned. "Eight hours? Why didn't you tell me?"

Her eyes began to tear again. "Because it would have ruined our plans. I wanted to be with you no matter what."

"Shh." Tiel patted her hand. "Crying will only make you feel worse. Think about the baby coming. It can't be much longer now." She looked across at Doc. "Can it?"

"Hard to say with first babies."

"Your best guess."

"Two, three hours." He stood up and faced off with Ronnie. "She's going to deliver tonight. How easy or difficult the labor and birth will be rests with you. She needs a hospital, a well-equipped delivery room, and medical personnel. The baby will also need attention immediately after it's born. That's the situation. What are you going to do about it?"

Sabra cried out with another pain. Doc dropped down beside her and monitored the contraction by placing his hands on her abdomen. The steep frown between his eyebrows alerted Tiel to trouble. "What?" she asked.

"Not good."

"*What?*"

He shook his head, indicating that he didn't want to discuss it in front of the girl. But Sabra Dendy was no dummy. She picked up on his concern. "Something's wrong, isn't it?"

To his credit, Doc didn't talk down to her. "Not wrong, Sabra. Just more complicated."

"What?"

"Do you know what breech means?"

Tiel's breath caught. She heard Gladys make a tsking sound of regret.

"That's when the baby..." Sabra paused to swallow hard. "When the baby is upside down."

He nodded solemnly. "I think your baby is in the wrong position. Its head isn't down."

She began to whimper. "What can you do?"

"Sometimes it isn't necessary to do anything. The baby will turn on its own."

"What's the worst that can happen?"

Doc looked up at Ronnie, who'd asked the question. "A cesarean section is done, sparing the mother and child a grueling delivery. A vaginal delivery is dangerous, and can be life-threatening. Knowing that, will you let someone call nine-one-one and get Sabra some help?"

"No!" the girl cried. "I won't go to a hospital. I won't!"

Doc took her hand. "Your baby could die, Sabra."

"You can help me."

"I'm not equipped."

"You can anyway. I know you can."

"Sabra, please listen to him," Tiel urged. "He knows what he's talking about. A breech birth would be extremely painful. It could also endanger your baby's life or cause serious defects. Please urge Ronnie to take Doc's advice. Let us call nine-one-one."

"No," she said, shaking her head stubbornly. "You don't understand. My daddy swore that neither I nor Ronnie would ever see our baby after it's born. He's going to give it away."

"I doubt if—"

But Sabra didn't allow Tiel to finish. "He said the baby would mean no more to him than an unwanted puppy he would take to the dog pound. When he says something, he means it. He'll take our baby, and we'll never see it. He'll keep us apart, too. He said he would, and he will." She began to sob.

"Oh, my," Gladys murmured. "Poor things."

Tiel glanced over her shoulder at the others. Vern and Gladys were sitting up now, huddled together, his arms protectively around her. Both were looking on sorrowfully.

The two Mexican men were talking softly together, their hostile eyes darting about. Tiel hoped they weren't plotting another attempt to overthrow Ronnie. Donna the cashier was still lying on the floor face-down, but she muttered, "Poor things, my ass. Almost killed me."

Ronnie, having reached a decision, looked at Doc and said, "Sabra wants you to help her."

He looked as though he were about to argue. Then, maybe because time was a factor, he changed his mind. "All right. For the time being, I'll do what I can, starting with an internal examination."

"You mean her ..."

"Yes. That's what I mean. I need to know how far the labor has progressed. Find something for me to sterilize my hands with."

"I've got some of that waterless hand wash," Tiel told him. "It's antibacterial."

"Good. Thanks."

She made to get up, but Ronnie halted her. "Get it and come right back. Remember, I'm watching."

She returned to the spot where she had dropped her satchel, her soft drinks, and her sunflower seeds. She retrieved the plastic container of hand wash from her satchel. Then, getting Vern's attention, she mimicked holding a video camera up to her eye. At first he looked perplexed, but then Gladys nudged him in the ribs and whispered in his ear. Nodding vigorously, he hitched his chin in the direction of the magazine rack. Tiel remembered they'd been browsing there when the robbery commenced.

She returned with the bottle of hand wash and handed it to Doc. "Shouldn't she have something beneath her?"

"We've got some bed pads in the RV."

"Gladys!" Vern exclaimed, obviously mortified by his wife's admission.

"They would be perfect," Tiel said, remembering the disposable protective pads she'd seen on Uncle Pete's bed in the nursing home. They prevented the staff from having to change the bed linens each time a resident had an accident. "I'll go get them."

"Like hell," Ronnie said, dashing that idea. "Not you. But the old man can go. She," he added, pointing the pistol at Gladys, "stays here."

Gladys patted Vern's bony knee. "I'll be fine, honey."

"You're sure? If anything happened to you..."

"Nothing is going to happen to me. That boy's got more than me to worry about."

Vern levered his rickety body up off the floor, dusted

off the seat of his shorts, and moved to the door. "Well, I can't walk through glass."

Ronnie nudged Donna again, who instantly began imploring him to spare her life. He instructed her to shut up and unlock the door, which she did.

At the door Ronnie and the elderly man exchanged a meaningful look. "Don't worry, I'll be back," the old man assured him. "I wouldn't do anything to jeopardize my wife's life." And, although Ronnie Davison was fifty pounds heavier and half a foot taller, he issued him a warning. "If you harm her, I'll kill you."

Ronnie pushed open the door and Vern slipped through. His attempt at a jog was unintentionally comical. Tiel watched his progress across the parking lot until he reached the gas pumps and climbed into the Winnebago.

Doc was talking Sabra through another pain. When it passed, the girl relaxed and closed her eyes. Tiel looked at Doc, who was watching the girl. "What else would be helpful to you?"

"Gloves."

"I'll see what I can find."

"Some vinegar."

"Standard distilled vinegar?"

"Hmm." After a brief pause, he remarked, "You're awfully cool under pressure."

"Thanks." They continued to watch the girl, who, for the moment, seemed to be asleep. Tiel asked softly, "Is this going to end badly?"

His lips compressed into a grim line. "Not if I can help it."

"How bad—"

"Hey, what are you two whispering about?"

Tiel looked up at Ronnie. "Doc needs some gloves. I was about to ask Donna if the store stocks them."

"Okay, go ahead."

She left Sabra's side and moved to the counter. Donna was standing behind it, waiting to unlock the door when Vern returned. She regarded Tiel suspiciously. "What do you want?"

"Donna, please remain calm. Hysteria will only worsen the situation. For the time being, we're all safe."

"Safe? Ha! This is my third time."

"To be robbed?"

"My luck's bound to run out. First time, there were three of them. Came in pretty as you please, emptied the register, and locked me in the freezer. If the dairy delivery man hadn't come by, I'd've been a goner. Second time, this guy in a mask clubbed me good 'longside the head with the butt of his pistol. Had a concussion and couldn't work for six weeks on account of headaches. So dizzy I puked 'round the clock." Her narrow chest rose and fell on a deep sigh of resignation. "It's only a matter o' time. The odds'll catch up with me, and one of 'em'll kill me. Do you think he'd let us smoke?"

"If you're so afraid, why don't you quit and get another job?"

She looked at Tiel as though she had lost her mind. "I love my work."

If that was logical, maybe Tiel *was* losing her mind. "Do you carry any latex gloves in the store? The kind a doctor wears."

She shook her frizzy, permed head. "Rubbermaid. That's it. I think we got two pairs over yonder with the household cleansers."

"Thanks. Stay cool, Donna."

As Tiel moved past Gladys, she leaned down and whispered, "Is there a tape in your video camera?"

The old lady nodded. "Two hours' worth. Rewound,

too. Unless Vern screwed it up when he was fiddling with it."

"If I can get it to you—"

"Hey!" Ronnie shouted. "What are you whispering about now?"

"She's afraid for her husband. I was reassuring her."

"There he is now," Gladys said, pointing at the door.

Donna threw the bolt and Vern came tottering in, everything except his spindly legs hidden behind a stack of bedding. Ronnie ordered him to drop the load of pillows and quilts, but the old man argued. "It's all clean. If I drop it, it'll get dirty. The lady should have a comfortable place to lie, and I thought these towels might come in handy, too."

"Actually that's very good thinking, Ronnie," Tiel said. "You can examine the stuff once he brings it over."

From his Winnebago, in addition to the pads he'd gone for, Vern had brought two pillows, two quilts, two clean bedsheets, and several bath towels. Ronnie found nothing concealed inside the linens and gave the go-ahead for Tiel to make a pallet, which she did while Sabra leaned heavily against Doc.

Tiel used only one of the sheets, saving the spare for later, should the need for it arise. When she was finished, Doc laid the girl down on the bedding. She settled on it gratefully. Tiel placed one of the disposal pads beneath her hips.

"They're not for what you think," Vern declared. Simultaneously Tiel and Doc glanced up at the old man, surprised to see him bending down to confide in them. "We're not incontinent."

Tiel could barely contain her smile. "We didn't ask."

"We're on our honeymoon," Vern explained in a

confidential whisper. "Every night we go at it. Daytime too, if the urge strikes us. You know how randy honeymooners are. Those pads aren't the most comfortable things for the partner on bottom, but neither of us likes to lie in the wet spot, and it beats changing the sheets after each time."

The old man winked, turned away, and obeyed Ronnie's instruction to rejoin the others. He sat down beside his wife—his bride—who hugged him and gave him a smacking kiss on the cheek, commending him for his bravery.

Tiel, realizing her jaw was hanging slack, closed it with a soft click of her teeth. Her gaze slid to Doc, who was intent on timing Sabra's labor pain, but his thin lips were twitching with a smile.

From beneath his eyebrows, he glanced up at Tiel, caught her looking at him, and made a snuffling sound that passed for a laugh. "Gloves?"

"What?"

"Did you ask about the gloves?"

"Oh, uh, two pair of Rubbermaid."

He shook his head. "Just as well be leather work gloves. What about some vinegar?"

"Coming up."

"And gauze."

She asked Ronnie's permission to shop the aisles, where she found several plastic bottles of vinegar, a box of sterile gauze pads, and a package of disposable baby wipes. She gathered them up. On her way back to Sabra, another display caught her eye. On a burst of inspiration, she added two boxes of hair coloring to her collection.

When she got back to the girl, Sabra was listening intently to what Doc was telling her.

"It won't be comfortable, but I'll try not to hurt you, okay?"

The girl nodded and glanced apprehensively at Tiel.

"Have you ever had a pelvic exam, Sabra?" she asked softly.

"Once. When I went for birth-control pills." Tiel cocked her head quizzically, and Sabra lowered her eyes in embarrassment. "I stopped taking them because they made me fat."

"I see. Well, you've been examined before, so you know what to expect. This probably won't be any worse than that first exam. Right, Doc?"

"I'll make it as easy as I can."

Tiel gave the girl's hand a quick squeeze. "I'll be right over there if you—"

"No, stay here with me. Please." She motioned Tiel down for a private consultation.

"He's nice," she said, speaking in a low voice directly into Tiel's ear. "He acts like a doctor, and talks like a doctor, but he doesn't look like one, know what I mean?"

"Yes, I know what you mean."

"So I feel sorta weird, having him...you know? Could you, like, help me take off my underpants?"

Tiel straightened and looked at Doc. "Could you give us a moment, please?"

"Sure."

"What's happening?" Ronnie wanted to know when Doc stood up.

"The lady needs some privacy. From me. And you."

"But I'm her boyfriend."

"Which is exactly why you're the last person she wants observing."

"He's right, Ronnie," Sabra said. "Please."

The boy moved away with Doc. Tiel lifted Sabra's skirt and helped as she awkwardly raised her hips and worked her underwear down her thighs.

"There we go," Tiel said gently, taking away the damp garment, which Sabra had balled up to the size of a Ping-Pong ball.

"I'm sorry it's all icky."

"Sabra, starting right now, you're to stop apologizing. I've never been in labor, but I'm sure I wouldn't approach it with near the dignity that you have. Are you more comfortable now?" Obviously not. She could tell by Sabra's grimace that she was in the throes of another pain. "Doc?"

He was there in an instant, pressing his hands on the mound of her stomach. "Sure wish he'd turn on his own."

"I'm hoping for a girl," Sabra told him on gasping breaths.

Doc smiled. "Really?"

"Ronnie would like a girl too."

"Daughters are great, all right."

Tiel stole a glance at him. Did he have daughters? she wondered. She'd taken him for a bachelor, a loner. Maybe because he looked like the Marlboro man. You never saw the Marlboro man with a wife and family in tow.

Perhaps...? Tiel couldn't shake the feeling that she'd seen Doc somewhere before. His resemblance to the rugged models in the cigarette ads must be why he looked vaguely familiar.

When the pain passed, Doc placed his hands on the girl's raised knees. "Try and relax as much as possible. And let me know if I'm hurting you, okay?"

"Oh, wait." Tiel reached for a box of hair coloring

and opened it. Reading Doc's inquisitive expression, she explained. "It comes with disposable gloves. They won't be great; they probably won't even fit," she added, glancing down at his manly hands, "but they might be better than nothing."

"Good thinking."

He peeled the plastic gloves off the sheet of waxed paper to which they were stuck and worked his hands into them. It was an O. J. Simpson fit and they looked clumsy, but he thanked Tiel, then once again assured Sabra that he would try his best not to make it too unpleasant.

"This might help." For modesty's sake, Tiel spread the second sheet over the girl's knees.

Doc gave her an approving glance. "Just relax, Sabra. It'll be over before you know it."

She took a deep breath and pinched her eyes shut.

"First I'm going to wash the area with one of these wipes. Then bathe it with some vinegar. It might be a little cold."

As he poured the vinegar over her, blotting at it with several of the gauze pads, he asked her how she was doing.

"Okay," she replied timorously.

Tiel found herself holding her own breath. "Breathe deeply, Sabra. It'll help you relax. Let's do it together. Big inhale. Now out." Upon penetration, Sabra flinched. Tiel said, "Again. Another deep breath in. Out. That's it. Not much longer now. You're doing great."

But she wasn't. Doc's expression told her as much. He withdrew his hand from between the girl's thighs and, hiding his concern, bragged on how well she'd done. He peeled off the gloves and reached for the bottle of hand wash, rubbing it vigorously onto his hands and forearms.

"Is everything all right?"

Ronnie was back. It was he who had asked the question, but Doc addressed his answer to Sabra. "You haven't dilated much."

"What does that mean?"

"It means that your labor is dysfunctional."

"Dysfunctional?"

"That's a harsh word, but that's the medical term for it. As hard and frequent as your pains are coming, your cervix should be dilated more than it is. The baby is trying to push its way out, but not all the parts of your body are ready for the birth."

"What can you do?"

"I can't do anything, Ronnie, but you can. You can stop this foolishness and get Sabra to a facility where she'll receive proper obstetric care."

"I already told you, no."

"No," Sabra repeated.

Before there could be any further argument, the telephone rang.

Chapter 4

The unexpected, shrill sound startled everyone.

Donna was nearest to the ringing telephone. "What should I do?" she asked.

"Nothing."

"Ronnie, maybe you should let her answer it," Tiel suggested.

"How come? It's probably got nothing to do with me."

"That could be. But what if it does concern you? Wouldn't you rather know what you're up against?"

He mulled it over for several seconds, then gave Donna the go-ahead to answer.

"Hello?" She listened for a moment, then said, "Hi, Sheriff. No, he weren't drunk. Just like he told you, this kid here has got us held at gunpoint."

Suddenly the front of the building was bathed in brilliant light. Everyone inside had been so focused on Sabra's condition that none had heard the approach of the three squad cars, which had now flashed on their headlights. Tiel deduced that the sheriff was probably

calling from one of the units, which were parked just beyond the gas pumps.

Ronnie ducked out of sight behind a Frito-Lay display, yelling, "Tell them to turn off those damn lights or
I'm going to shoot somebody."

Donna relayed the message. She paused to listen,
then said, "About eighteen, I'd guess. Calls hisself Ronnie."

"Shut up!" Ronnie brandished the pistol at her. She
screeched and dropped the telephone receiver.

The car lights went out, two pair almost simultaneously, the third pair seconds later.

Sabra moaned.

Doc said, "Ronnie, listen to me."

"No. Be quiet and let me think."

The young man was flustered, but Doc persisted in a
low, earnest voice. "Stay here and see this thing through
if you like. But the manly thing to do would be to let
Sabra leave. The authorities will take her to the hospital, where she needs to be."

"I won't go," the girl said. "Not without Ronnie."

Tiel appealed to her. "Think of your baby, Sabra."

"I am thinking of our baby," she sobbed. "If my
daddy gets his hands on the baby, I'll never see it again.
I won't give it up. I won't give Ronnie up, either."

Seeing that his patient was close to hysteria, Doc relented. "Okay, okay. If you won't agree to leave, how
about this? What if a doctor were to come here?"

"You're a doctor," Ronnie argued.

"Not the kind Sabra needs. I don't have any in-
struments. I've got nothing to give her to relieve her
pain. This is going to be a difficult delivery, Ronnie. There could be all sorts of serious complications,
which I'm unqualified to deal with. Are you willing

to risk Sabra's life as well as the child's? Because by allowing the situation to continue as it is, that's what you're doing. You could lose one or both of them. Then, no matter how it pans out, it will all have been for nothing."

Tiel was impressed. She couldn't have phrased an appeal any better.

The young man gnawed on Doc's words for a minute, then motioned Tiel toward the counter and the dangling telephone receiver. For several moments after Donna had dropped it, a man's voice could be heard, demanding to know what was going on. Now, it was silent.

"You're good at shooting off your mouth," Ronnie said to Tiel. "You do the talking."

She came to her feet and made her way past Sabra and Doc, past the Frito-Lay display and across the open space to the counter. She wasted no time calling nine-one-one. As soon as the operator answered, she said, "I need the sheriff to call me. Don't ask questions. He is aware of this emergency situation. Tell him to call the convenience store back." She hung up before the operator could proceed with the routine drill, which would be a waste of valuable time.

They waited in tense silence. No one said a word. Gladys and Vern were huddled close together. When Tiel glanced in their direction, Vern subtly drew her attention to the tote bag in his lap. Somehow he had managed to retrieve it without Ronnie's being aware. A crafty Casanova. That in itself would make a good story, Tiel thought. Except that she had a better one, in which she wasn't just a reporter, but a participant. Gully would be ecstatic. If this story didn't secure the *Nine Live* spot for her—

Although she'd been expecting the telephone to ring, she jumped when it did. She answered it immediately.

"Who's this?"

She avoided a direct answer by saying, "Sheriff?"

"Marty Montez."

"Sheriff Montez, I've been appointed spokesperson. I'm one of the hostages."

"Are you in immediate danger?"

"No," she replied, believing it.

"Are you being coerced?"

"No."

"Give me a rundown."

She began with a brief and concise account of the robbery, starting with Ronnie's shooting out the security camera. "It was interrupted when his accomplice went into labor."

"Labor? You mean labor like having a baby?"

"Exactly like that, yes."

After an extended pause during which she could hear the heavy breathing of an overweight man, he said, "Answer me if you safely can, miss. Are these robbers by any chance a coupla high school kids?"

"Yes."

"What's he asking?" Ronnie demanded to know.

Tiel covered the receiver with her palm. "He asked if Sabra was in pain and I answered."

"Jee-sus," the sheriff exclaimed in a near whistle. In a low voice he passed along to his deputies—or so Tiel assumed—that the hostage-takers were the kids "outta Fort Worth." Then to her, he asked, "Is anybody hurt?"

"No. We're all unharmed."

"Who-all's in there with you? How many hostages?"

"Four men and two women besides myself."

"You're a smooth talker. You wouldn't by any chance be a Ms. McCoy?"

She tried to hide her surprise from Ronnie, who was listening to her intently and closely monitoring her facial expressions. "That's correct. No one has been wounded."

"You are Ms. McCoy, but you don't want 'em to know you're a TV reporter? I see. Your boss, guy name o' Gully, he's called my office twice, demanding we put out an APB for you. Said you started from Rojo Flats and was supposed to call him—"

"What's he saying?" Ronnie asked.

She interrupted the sheriff. "It would be in everyone's best interest if you could provide us with a doctor. An OB if possible."

"Tell him to bring along anything he might need for a difficult delivery."

Tiel relayed Doc's message.

"Be sure he knows that the baby is in a breech position," Doc added.

After Tiel conveyed that, the sheriff asked who she was getting her information from. "He goes by Doc."

"You're shittin' me," the sheriff said.

"No."

"Doc's one of the hostages," she heard him pass along. "Doc says the Dendy girl needs a specialist, huh?"

"That's right, Sheriff. And as soon as possible. We're concerned for her and the baby."

"If they surrender, we'll get her to a hospital pronto. They have my guarantee."

"I'm afraid that's not a contingency."

"Davison won't let her go?"

"No," Tiel said. "She refuses to leave."

"Shee-ut, what a mess," he expelled on a heavy sigh. "Okay, I'll see what I can do."

"Sheriff, I can't impress on you enough how badly this young woman is suffering. And..."

"Go ahead, Ms. McCoy. What?"

"The situation is under control," she said slowly. "For the time being everyone is calm. Please don't take any drastic measures."

"I hear what you're saying, Ms. McCoy. No grandstanding. No fireworks, SWAT teams, and such?"

"Precisely." She was relieved that he understood. "So far, no one has been injured."

"And we'd all like to keep it that way."

"I'm very glad to hear you say that. Please, please, get a doctor here as quickly as you can."

"I'm on it. Here's the number of the phone I've got with me."

She committed the number to memory. Montez wished her luck and hung up. She replaced the telephone on the countertop, glad to note that it was an older model and didn't have a speaker-phone feature. Ronnie might wish to listen in on future conversations.

"He's working on getting a doctor here."

"I like the sound of that," Doc said.

"How soon before he gets here?"

Turning to Ronnie, she replied, "As soon as possible. I'm going to be honest with you. He guessed your and Sabra's identity."

"Oh, hell," the boy groaned. "What else can go wrong?"

"They've been located!"

Russell Dendy nearly knocked down the FBI agent who happened to be standing in his path when the shout came from the adjacent room. He didn't apologize for causing the agent to spill scalding coffee over his hand. He barreled into the library of his home, which, since that morning, had been converted into a command post.

"Where? Where are they? Has he hurt my daughter? Is Sabra all right?"

Special Agent William Calloway was in charge. He was a tall, thin, balding man who, if not for the pistol riding in the small of his back, looked more like a mortgage banker than a federal agent. His demeanor wasn't consistent with the stereotype either. He was calm and soft-spoken—most of the time. Russell Dendy had put Calloway's pleasant disposition to the test.

As Dendy stalked into the room blurting questions, Calloway signaled for him to pipe down and continued his telephone conversation.

Dendy impatiently punched a button on the telephone and a woman's voice filtered through the speaker. "It's called Rojo Flats. Practically in the middle of nowhere, west-southwest of San Angelo. They're armed. They tried to rob a convenience store, but it was thwarted. Now they're holding hostages inside the store."

"Damn him. Damn him!" Dendy ground his fist into his opposite palm. "He turned my daughter into a common criminal! And she couldn't understand why I objected to him."

Calloway once again signaled him to keep his voice down. "You said they're armed. Are there any casualties?"

"No, sir. But the girl is in labor."

"Inside the store?"

"Affirmative."

Dendy cursed lavishly. "He's holding her against her will!"

The disembodied woman said, "According to one of the hostages who spoke to the sheriff, the young woman refuses to leave."

"He's brainwashed her," Dendy declared.

The FBI agent from the Odessa office continued as though she hadn't heard him. "One of the hostages apparently has some medical knowledge. He's seeing to her, but a doctor has been requested."

Dendy thumped the top of the desk with his fist. "I want Sabra the hell out of there, do you hear me?"

"We hear you, Mr. Dendy," Calloway said with diminishing patience.

"I don't care if you have to blast her out of there with dynamite."

"Well, I care. According to the spokesperson, no one has been injured."

"My daughter's in labor!"

"And we'll get her to a hospital as soon as possible. But I'm not going to do anything that will endanger the lives of those hostages, your daughter, or Mr. Davison."

"Look, Calloway, if you're going to take a limp-dick approach to this situation—"

"The approach I take is my call, not yours. Is that understood?"

Russell Dendy had the reputation of being a real son of a bitch. Unfortunately, meeting him hadn't dispelled any myths or changed Calloway's preconceptions of the millionaire.

Dendy exercised despotic supervision over several

corporations. He wasn't accustomed to relinquishing control to someone else, or even to giving anyone else a vote in the way things were managed. His businesses weren't democracies, and neither was his family. Mrs. Dendy had done nothing all day except weep into her hankie and second her husband's answers to the agents' probing questions about their family life and their relationship with their daughter. She hadn't offered a single opinion that differed from his, or voiced any personal observations.

From the start Calloway had doubted Dendy's allegation of a kidnaping. Instead he leaned heavily toward the more viable version: Sabra Dendy had run away from home with her boyfriend in order to escape her domineering father.

Calloway's dressing-down had left Russ Dendy practically spitting with fury. "I'm on my way out there."

"I don't advise that."

"As if I give a rat's ass what you advise."

"There's no room in our chopper for extra passengers," the agent called to Dendy's retreating back.

"Then I'll take my Lear."

He stormed from the room and began shouting orders to his band of flunkies who were ever present, as silent and unobtrusive as pieces of furniture until Dendy's strident commands jump-started them. They filed out behind him. Mrs. Dendy was ignored and not invited to go along.

Calloway disengaged the speaker phone and picked up the receiver, so he could hear the other agent more clearly. "Guess you heard all that."

"You've got your hands full, Calloway."

"And then some. How're the locals out there?"

"From what I understand, Montez is a competent

sheriff, but he's in way over his head and is smart
enough to know it. He's getting backup from the
Rangers and highway patrol."

"Will they resent our presence, you think?"

"Don't they always?" she came back dryly.

"Well, it came to us as a kidnaping. I'm leaving it at
that until I know better."

"Actually, Montez will probably be glad to land the
problem in our lap. His chief concern is that there be no
heroics. He wants to avoid bloodshed."

"Then he and I are on the same page. I think what
we've got here is a couple of scared kids who've got
themselves trapped in a situation and can't find a way
out. What, if anything, do you know about the
hostages?"

She gave him the breakdown by gender. "One's been
identified by Sheriff Montez as a local rancher. The
cashier is a fixture at the convenience store. Everybody
in Rojo Flats knows her. And that Ms. McCoy who
talked to Sheriff Montez?"

"What about her?"

"She's a reporter for a TV station in Dallas."

"Tiel McCoy?"

"So you know her?"

He knew her and mentally formed an image: slender,
short blond hair, light eyes. Blue, possibly green. She
was on TV nearly every night. Calloway had also seen
her outside the studio among reporters at the scenes of
crimes he'd investigated. She was aggressive, but objec-
tive. Her reports were never unfairly inflammatory or
exploitative. She was a looker and utterly feminine, but
her delivery merited credibility.

He wasn't thrilled to hear that a broadcast journalist of her caliber was at the epicenter of this crisis. It

was a compounding factor he could easily have done without.

"Great. A reporter is already on the scene." He ran his hand around the back of his neck, where tension had begun to gather. It was going to be a long night. He predicted the previously unheard-of Rojo Flats would soon be swarmed by media, contributing to the mayhem.

The other agent asked, "Gut instinct, Calloway. Did that boy kidnap the Dendy girl?"

Beneath his breath, Calloway muttered, "I only wonder why it took her so long to run away."

Chapter 5

While they waited for the promised doctor to arrive, Doc gleaned a pair of scissors and a pair of shoelaces from the store's stock. He placed them to boil in a carafe usually used for water with which to mix instant hot drinks. He also took from the shelves sanitary napkins, adhesive tape, and a box of plastic trash bags.

He asked Donna if they stocked aspirators. When she stared at him blankly, he explained. "A rubber bulb syringe. To suck the mucus from the baby's nose and throat."

She scratched her scaly elbow. "Don't have much call for those."

Ronnie was nervous when Doc picked up the carafe of boiling water. He ordered him to let Gladys pour out the water, which the elderly lady was all too happy to do.

Following that activity, the wait grew to be interminable. Everyone inside the store was aware of the increasing number of arriving vehicles. The distance be-

tween the gasoline pumps and the store's entrance was
like a DMZ; it was kept clear. But the area between the
pumps and the highway became congested with official and emergency vehicles. When that space was filled,
they began parking on the shoulder of the highway, lin-
ing both sides of the state road. They hadn't arrived
running hot, but the absence of flashing lights and sirens
made their presence even more ominous.

Tiel wondered if the back of the building was seeing
as much activity as the front. Obviously that possibility
occurred to Ronnie, too, because he asked Donna about
a rear door.

She said, "In the hall going to the bathrooms? See
that door? Through that is the stockroom. Also the
freezer where those crazy kids locked me in."

"I asked about the back door."

"It's steel and bolted from the inside. It has a bar
acrost it, and the hinges are on the inside, too. It's so
heavy I can barely open it for deliveries."

If Donna were telling the truth, no one would be
coming through the rear door silently. Ronnie would be
signaled of an attempt well ahead of time.

"What about the rest rooms?" he wanted to know.
"Any windows in them?"

She shook her head no.

"It's true," Gladys chirped. "I was in the ladies'. If
you ask me, better ventilation wouldn't hurt."

Those worries laid to rest, Ronnie divided his attention among Sabra, his hostages, and the increasing
movement outside, which was more than enough to
keep him occupied. Tiel excused herself from Sabra's
side and asked Ronnie if she could get into her satchel.
"My contacts are dry. I need my wetting solution."

He glanced quickly toward the bag where it sat on

top of the counter. She'd left it there after retrieving the hand wash for Doc. He seemed to be debating the advisability of granting her permission when she said, "It won't take a sec. I can't be away from Sabra long. She likes having another woman nearby."

"Okay. But I'm watching you. Don't think I'm not."

The young man's bravado was affected. He was scared and frazzled, but he still had his finger on the trigger of the pistol. Tiel didn't want to be the one responsible for sending him over the edge.

She moved to the counter where Ronnie could see her digging into her satchel in search of the small vial of solution. She uncapped it and tilted her head back to apply the drops. "Damn," she cursed softly, holding a finger over her eye. She then removed her contact lens, dug around in the bag for another bottle of solution and proceeded to clean the lens in a small pool of solution in her palm.

Without turning to look at Gladys and Vern, she spoke to them in a whisper. "Does your camera have a tape in it?"

Vern—bless him—was inspecting a loose cuticle on his left hand and looking about as conspiratorial as an altar boy. "Yes, ma'am."

"Fresh batteries too," Gladys added as she folded her crew sock down to form a cuff around her ankle. She inspected it, then, deciding she liked it better the other way, rolled it back up. "It's all set to go. Get ready. We've got a distraction planned."

"Wait—"

Before Tiel could finish, Vern went into a fit of coughing. Gladys leaped up, tossed their tote bag onto the counter within Tiel's reach, then started whacking her husband hard between his shoulder blades.

"Oh, Lord, Vern, not one of your strangling spells. Of all times to get choked on your own spit. For mercy's sake!"

Tiel popped in her contact and blinked it into place. Then, as everyone including Ronnie was watching the old man gasp and gurgle in an effort to regain his breath while Gladys smacked away as though beating a rug, she reached into the tote bag for the camera.

She was familiar enough with home recorders to know where the power switch was located. She flipped it on and punched the Record button. She then set it on a shelf, wedging it between cartons of cigarettes and praying it wouldn't be noticed. She didn't have high hopes for the quality of the picture, but amateur videos had proved invaluable in the past, including the Zapruder film of JFK's assassination and the disturbing video of the Rodney King beating in Los Angeles.

Vern's coughs subsided. Gladys asked Ronnie's permission to get a bottle of water for him.

Tiel replaced the contact-lens cleaner and wetting solution in her bag and was about to withdraw her hand when she spotted her audiocassette recorder. She sometimes used the minuscule recorder during interviews as a supplement to the video recording. Later, when writing her script, she didn't have to sit in an editing booth and watch the video in order to hear the interview. She could replay it on the tiny recorder.

She hadn't intentionally brought it along. It was a tool of her trade, not a vacation item. But there it was, buried in the bottom of her bag, looking to her like a broadcast news icon waiting to be excavated. She imagined it radiating a shimmering, golden aura.

She palmed the recording device and slipped it into the pocket of her slacks just as Sabra gave a sharp cry.

Frantically, Ronnie looked around for Tiel. "I'm coming," she told him.

Giving the elderly thespians a thumbs-up as she stepped around them, she rushed back to Sabra's side.

Doc looked worried. "Her pains have slowed down somewhat, but when she has one it's acute. Where the hell is that doctor? What's taking so long?"

Tiel blotted Sabra's sweating forehead with a pad of gauze she had moistened with cool drinking water. "When he—or she—does get here, how effective can he be? What will he be able to do under these circumstances?"

"Let's just hope he has some experience with breech births. Or maybe he'll be able to convince Ronnie and Sabra that a C-section is mandatory."

"And if neither is the case...?"

"It will be bad," he said grimly. "For all concerned."

"Can you do without a bulb syringe?"

"Hopefully the doctor will bring one. He should."

"What if she hasn't dilated...?"

"I'm counting on nature taking its course. Maybe the baby will turn on its own. That happens."

Tiel stroked the girl's head. Sabra appeared to be dozing. The final stages of labor hadn't even begun, and already she was exhausted. "It's good she can take these short naps."

"Her body knows that later it'll need all the strength it can muster."

"I wish she didn't have to suffer."

"Suffering is a bitch, all right," he said, almost to himself. "The doctor can give her an injection to relieve the pain. Something that won't harm the fetus. But only up to a point. The closer she gets to delivery, the greater the risk of giving her drugs."

"What about a spinal? Don't they administer that in the final stages of labor?"

"I doubt he'll try to do a block under these conditions, although he might feel confident enough."

After a moment of thought, Tiel said, "I think going the natural route is nuts. I guess that makes me a disgrace to womankind."

"You have children?" When his eyes connected with hers, it felt like she had been poked lightly just below her navel.

"Uh, no." She quickly lowered her gaze from his. "I'm just saying that if and when I ever do, I want drugs with a capital *D*."

"I understand completely."

And Tiel got the impression that he did. When she looked at him again, he had returned his attention to Sabra. "Do you have children, Doc?"

"No."

"Earlier you made a comment about daughters that led me to think—"

"No." His fingers loosely encircled Sabra's wrist, as his thumb pressed her pulse point. "I wish I had a blood-pressure cuff. And surely he'll bring a fetoscope."

"That..."

"Monitors the fetal heartbeat. Hospitals now use fancy ultrasound devices. But I'd settle for a fetoscope."

"Where did you get your medical training?"

"What really concerns me," he said, ignoring her question, "is whether or not he'll perform an episiotomy."

Tiel winced at the thought of the incision and the delicate area subjected to it. "How could he?"

"It won't be pleasant, but if he doesn't, she could easily tear and that'll be even more unpleasant."

"You're doing my nerves no good, Doc."

"I imagine all our nerves have had better days." Again he raised his head and looked across at her. "By the way, I'm glad you're here."

The look was just as intense, the eyes as compelling, as before, but this time she didn't chicken out and look away. "I'm not doing anything constructive."

"Simply being with her is doing a lot. When she's having a pain, encourage her not to fight it. Tensing the muscles and tissue surrounding the uterus only increases the discomfort. The uterus was made to contract. She should let it go about its business."

"Easy for you to say."

"Easy for me to say," he conceded with a wry smile. "Breathe with her. Take deep breaths inhaled through the nose, exhaled through the mouth."

"Those deep breaths will help me, too."

"You're doing fine. She feels comfortable with you. You neutralize her shyness."

"She admitted to being shy with you."

"Understandable. She's very young."

"She said you don't look like a doctor."

"No, I don't suppose I do."

"Are you?"

"Rancher."

"You're a real cowboy then?"

"I breed horses, run a herd of beef cattle. I drive a pickup truck. I guess that makes me a cowboy."

"Then where'd you learn—"

The ringing of the telephone brought their private conversation to a halt. Ronnie snatched up the receiver. "Hello? I'm Ronnie Davison. Where's the doctor?"

He paused to listen, and Tiel could tell by his expression that he was hearing something that distressed him.

"FBI? How come?" Then he blurted, "But I didn't kidnap her, Mr. Calloway! We were eloping. Yes, sir, she's my main concern too. No. No. She refuses to go to a hospital."

He listened longer, then glanced at Sabra. "Okay. If the phone'll reach." He dragged the telephone to Sabra, stretching the cord as far as it would go. "The FBI agent wants to talk to you."

Doc said, "It won't hurt her to stand up. In fact, it might do her good."

He and Tiel supported Sabra beneath the arms and together assisted her to her feet. She baby-stepped far enough to take the extended receiver from Ronnie.

"Hello? No, sir. What Ronnie told you is true. I'm not leaving without him. Not even to go to the hospital. Because of my daddy! He said he'll take away my baby, and he always does what he says." She sniffed back tears. "Of course I came with Ronnie voluntarily. I—" She caught her breath and gripped a handful of Doc's shirt.

He lifted her and carried her back to the makeshift birthing bed, depositing her gently. Tiel knelt beside her and, as Doc had instructed, coaxed Sabra to relax, not to fight the contraction, and to breathe.

Ronnie was speaking anxiously into the telephone. "Listen here, Mr. Calloway, Sabra can't talk anymore. She's having a contraction. Where's the doctor we were promised?" He glanced through the plate glass. "Yeah, I see him. You bet I'll let him in."

Ronnie slammed down the receiver and dropped the phone back onto the counter. He started for the door, then, realizing how exposed he would be to sharpshooters, ducked behind the Frito-Lay display again. "Cashier, wait until he's at the door before you unlock it. Then, as soon as he comes through, relock it. Understand?"

"What d'ya think, I'm stupid?"

Donna waited until the doctor was pushing on the door before she flipped the switch. He came inside, and everyone in the store, including the young doctor, heard the metallic click when the door relocked.

Nervously he glanced over his shoulder at it before introducing himself. "I'm, uh, Dr. Cain. Scott."

"Move over here."

Dr. Scott Cain was a handsome man of medium height and build, in his early to mid-thirties. Wide-eyed, he scanned the people huddled in a group in front of the counter. Gladys waved at him.

His gaze swung back to Ronnie. "I was making my rounds at County when I was paged. Never would've guessed I'd be called in on an emergency like this."

"With all due respect, Dr. Cain, we're short on time."

Tiel shared Doc's impatience. The wet-behind-the-ears Dr. Cain was obviously awed to find himself a player in such high drama. He hadn't fully grasped the seriousness of the situation.

Doc asked if he'd been apprised of Sabra's condition.

"I was told she was in labor and that there might be complications."

Doc motioned him toward the prone girl. "Is it okay?" Cain asked Ronnie, glancing fearfully at the pistol.

"Open up your bag."

"Huh? Oh, sure." He unlatched the black valise and held it open for Ronnie's inspection.

"Okay, go ahead. Help her, please. She's in a bad way."

"It would seem so," the doctor remarked as a contraction seized Sabra and she moaned.

Reflexively she reached for Tiel's hand. Tiel held on tight and spoke to her encouragingly. "The doctor's here, Sabra. Things are going to get better now. I promise."

Doc was providing the doctor with pertinent information. "She's seventeen. This is her first child. First pregnancy." They took up positions near the girl, Doc on Sabra's right side, Dr. Cain at her feet, Tiel on her left.

"How long has she been in labor?"

"Preliminary contractions started midafternoon. Her water broke about two hours ago. Pains escalated sharply after that, then for the last half hour they've tapered off."

"Hi, Sabra," the doctor said to the girl.

"Hi."

He placed his hands on her stomach and examined the mound with light, massaging squeezes.

"Breech, right?" Doc asked, seeking confirmation of his diagnosis.

"Right."

"Do you think you can turn the fetus?"

"That's very tricky."

"Do you have experience in breech births?"

"I've assisted."

That wasn't the hoped-for answer. Doc asked, "Did you bring a blood-pressure cuff?"

"In my bag."

The doctor continued to examine Sabra by gently probing her abdomen. Doc extended the blood-pressure cuff to him, but he declined to take it. He was speaking to Sabra. "Just relax, and everything will be all right."

She glanced at Ronnie and smiled hopefully. "How long before the baby comes, Dr. Cain?"

"That's hard to say. Babies have a mind of their own. I would prefer taking you to the hospital while there's still time."

"No."

"It would be much safer for you and the baby."

"I can't leave on account of my father."

"He's very worried about you, Sabra. In fact, he's outside. He told me to tell you—"

Her whole body jerked as though having a muscle spasm. "Daddy's here?" Her voice was high, thin, panicked. "Ronnie?"

The news upset him as much as it had Sabra. "How'd he get here?"

Tiel patted the girl's shoulder. "It's okay. Don't think about your father now. Think about your baby. That's all you should be concerned with. Everything else will work out."

Sabra began to cry.

Doc leaned toward the doctor and whispered angrily, "Why'n hell did you tell her that? Couldn't that news have waited?"

Dr. Cain looked confused. "I thought she would be comforted to know that her father was here. They didn't have time to fill me in on all the details of the situation. I didn't know that information was going to upset her."

Doc looked ready to throttle him, and Tiel shared the impulse.

Doc was so angry his thin lips barely moved when he spoke. But knowing that any outward display of anger would only make the situation worse, he remained focused on the business at hand. "She hadn't dilated much when I examined her." Glancing at his wristwatch, he added, "But it's been over an hour since I did the internal."

The doctor nodded. "How much? Was she dilated, I mean."

"About eight, ten centimeters."

"Hmm."

"You son of a bitch."

Doc's low growl brought Tiel's head up with a snap. Had she heard him correctly? Apparently so, because Dr. Cain was regarding him with consternation.

"Son of a bitch!" Doc repeated, this time in an angry exclamation.

What happened next was forever thereafter a blur in Tiel's memory. She could never accurately remember the rapid sequence of events, but any recollection of them always made her hungry for chili.

Chapter 6

⸺◦《◉》◦⸺

The FBI van parked on the apron of concrete between the highway and the fuel pumps was equipped with high-tech paraphernalia used for deployment, surveillance, and communication. It was a rolling command post out of Midland-Odessa that had been mobilized and driven to Rojo Flats. It had arrived within minutes of Calloway's chopper from Fort Worth.

There wasn't an airstrip in the immediate area that would accommodate an airplane larger than a crop duster. Dendy's private jet had flown to Odessa, where a charter helicopter had been standing by to whisk him to the small town. Upon his arrival, he had barged his way into the van, demanding to know exactly what the situation was and how Calloway planned to remedy it.

Dendy had made a general nuisance of himself, and Calloway had had all he could stomach of the millionaire even before Dendy began grilling him over the maneuver presently under way.

Every eye was on the television monitor, which was

transmitting a live picture from a camera outside. They watched Cain enter the store, where he stood with his back to the door for a time before disappearing from view.

"What if it doesn't work?" Dendy asked. "What then?"

" 'What then' will depend on the outcome."

"You mean you don't have a contingency plan in place? What kind of outfit are you running here, Calloway?"

They squared off. The other men in the van stood by expectantly, waiting to see who detonated first, Dendy or Calloway. Ironically, it was a statement from Sheriff Marty Montez that defused the explosive tension.

He said, "I can save you both the suspense and tell you right now that it's not going to work."

As a courtesy—and also a smart diplomatic move—Agent Calloway had invited the county sheriff to join the top-level powwow.

"Doc's no fool," Montez continued. "You're asking for trouble, sending that rookie in there."

"Thank you, Sheriff Montez," Calloway said stiffly.

Then, as though Montez's statement had been prophetic, they heard gunshots. Two came a millisecond apart, one more several seconds later. The first two caused them all to freeze in place. The third galvanized them. Everyone inside the van went into motion and began speaking at once.

"Christ!" Dendy bellowed.

The camera was showing them nothing. Calloway grabbed a headset so he could hear the communiqués between the men in position in front of the store.

"Were those gunshots?" Dendy asked. "What's happening, Calloway? You said my daughter wouldn't be in any danger!"

Over his shoulder, Calloway shouted, "Sit down and be quiet, Mr. Dendy, or I'm going to have you physically removed from this van."

"If you fuck this up, I'll have *you* physically removed from this *planet!*"

Calloway's face turned white with wrath. "Careful, sir. You just threatened the life of a federal officer." He ordered one of his subordinate agents to remove Dendy.

He needed to know immediately who inside the store had fired at whom and whether anyone had been injured or killed. While he was trying to find out, he didn't need Dendy yelling threats at him.

Dendy boomed, "Like hell I'm leaving!"

Calloway left the overwrought father to his subordinates and turned back to the console, demanding information of the agents outside.

Tiel had watched with disbelief as Dr. Scott Cain yanked a pistol from an ankle holster and pointed it at Ronnie. "FBI! Drop the weapon!"

Sabra had screamed.

Doc had continued to swear at Cain. "All this time we've been waiting on a *doctor!*" he shouted. "Instead we get you! What kind of stupid stunt is this?"

Tiel had surged to her feet, begging, "No, please no. Don't shoot." She had feared she was about to see Ronnie Davison blown away right before her eyes.

"You're not a doctor?" the frantic young man had shrieked. "They promised us a doctor. Sabra needs a doctor."

"Drop your weapon, Davison! Now!"

"God dammit, all this time's been wasted." The veins

in Doc's neck had bulged with anger. If the agent hadn't been holding a pistol, Tiel guessed that Doc would have taken him by the throat. "That girl's in trouble. Life-threatening trouble. Don't any of you federal bastards get it?"

"Ronnie, do as he says," Tiel had implored. "Surrender. Please."

"No, Ronnie, don't!" Sabra had sobbed. "Daddy's out there."

"Why don't you both put down your pistols." Although Doc's chest had been rising and falling with agitation, he had regained some composure. "Nobody has to get hurt. We can all be reasonable, can't we?"

"No." Ronnie, resolute, had clutched the pistol grip tighter. "Mr. Dendy will have me arrested. I'll never see Sabra again."

"He's right," the girl had said.

"Maybe not," Doc had argued. "Maybe—"

"I'm giving you to the count of three to drop your weapon!" Cain had shouted, his voice cracking. He, too, it seemed, was cracking under pressure.

"Why'd you have to do this?" Ronnie had yelled at him.

"One."

"Why'd you trick us? My girlfriend is suffering. She needs a doctor. Why'd you do this?"

Tiel hadn't liked the way Ronnie's index finger was tensing around the trigger.

"Two."

"I said no! I won't give her up to Mr. Dendy."

Just as Cain had shouted "Three" and fired his pistol, Tiel grabbed a can of Wolf brand chili from the shelf nearest her and clouted him over the head with it.

He had dropped like a sack of cement. His shot went wide of his target, which had been Ronnie's chest, but it came within a hair's-breadth of Doc before striking the counter.

Reflexively Ronnie had fired his gun. The only damage that bullet did was to knock a chunk of plaster out of the far wall.

Donna had screamed, hit the floor, and covered her head with her hands, then continued screaming.

In the resulting confusion, the Mexican men had surged forward, nearly trampling Vern and Gladys in their haste.

Tiel, realizing that they intended to take the agent's pistol, had kicked it beneath a freezer chest out of reach.

"Get back! Get back!" Ronnie had shouted at them. He fired again for emphasis, but aimed well above their heads. The bullet pinged into an air-conditioning vent, but it stopped their rush toward him.

Now they all remained in a frozen tableau, waiting to see what happened next, who would be the first to move, to speak.

It turned out to be Doc. "Do as he says," he ordered the two Mexicans. He held up his left hand, palm out, signaling them to move back. His right hand was clamped over his left shoulder. Blood leaked through his fingers.

"You're shot!" Tiel exclaimed.

Ignoring her, he reasoned with the two Mexican men, who were obviously reluctant to comply. "If you go charging through that door, you're liable to get a belly full of bullets."

The language as well as the logic escaped them. They understood only Doc's insistence that they remain where they were. They rebuked him in rapid-fire Spanish. Tiel picked up the word *madre* several times. She could only imagine the rest. However, the two did as

Doc asked and skulked back to their original positions, muttering to each other and throwing hostile glares all around. Ronnie kept his pistol trained on them.

Donna was making more racket than Sabra, who was clenching her teeth to keep from crying out as a labor pain seized her. Doc ordered the cashier to stop making the god-awful noise.

"I'm not gonna live to see morning," she wailed.

"The way our luck's going, you probably will," Gladys snapped. "Now *shut up*."

As though her mouth had been corked, Donna's crying ceased instantly.

"Hang in there, sweetheart." Tiel had resumed her place at Sabra's side and was holding her hand through the contraction.

"I knew..." Sabra paused to pant several times. "I knew Daddy wouldn't leave it alone. I knew he would track us down."

"Don't think about him now."

"How is she?" Doc asked, joining them.

Tiel looked at his shoulder. "Are you hurt?"

He shook his head. "The bullet only grazed me. It stings, that's all." Through the tear in his sleeve, he swabbed the wound with a gauze pad, then covered it with another and asked Tiel to cut off a strip of adhesive tape. While he held the square in place, she secured it with the tape.

"Thanks."

"You're welcome."

Up to this point no one had given any attention to the unconscious man. Ronnie approached, transferring his pistol from one hand to the other and drying his damp palms alternately on the seat of his jeans. He hitched his chin toward Cain. "What about him?"

Tiel considered that a very good question. "I'll probably get years in prison for doing that."

Doc said to Ronnie, "I recommend that you let me drag him outside, so his buddies in that bad-ass van out there will know he's alive. If they think he's dead or wounded, it could get ugly, Ronnie."

Ronnie apprehensively glanced toward the outside and gnawed on his lower lip while considering the suggestion. "No, no." He looked over at Vern and Gladys, who seemed to be having as good a time as two people on a theme-park thrill ride. "Find some duct tape," Ronnie told them. "I'm sure the store sells it. Bind his hands and feet."

"If you do that, you'll only be digging yourself in deeper, son," Doc warned gently.

"I don't think I could get in any deeper."

Ronnie's expression was sad, as though he was just now fully comprehending the enormity of his predicament. What might have seemed a romantic adventure when he and Sabra ran away had turned into an incident involving the FBI and gunplay. He had committed several felonies. He was in serious trouble, and he was intelligent enough to know it.

The elderly couple stepped over the unconscious agent. Each took an ankle. It was an effort for them, but they were able to drag him away from Sabra, giving Doc and Tiel more room in which to function.

"They're going to lock me up forever," Ronnie continued. "But I want Sabra to be safe. I want her old man's promise that he'll let her keep our baby."

"Then let's end this here and now."

"I can't, Doc. Not before getting that guarantee from Mr. Dendy."

Doc motioned down to Sabra, who was panting through another pain with Tiel. "In the meantime—"

"We stay right here," the boy insisted.

"But she needs a—"

"Doc?" Tiel said, interrupting.

"—hospital. And soon. If you're truly worried about Sabra's welfare—"

"Doc?"

Irritated because she had twice interrupted his earnest appeal, he turned to her abruptly and asked impatiently, "What?"

"Sabra can't go anywhere. I can see the baby."

He knelt down between Sabra's raised knees. "Thank God," he said on a relieved laugh. "The baby's turned, Sabra. I can see the head. You're crowning. A few minutes from now you'll have a baby."

The girl laughed, sounding too young to be in the jam she was in. "Is it going to be all right?"

"I think so." Doc looked at Tiel. "You'll help?"

"Tell me what to do."

"Get a few more of those pads and spread them around her. Have one of the towels handy to wrap the baby in." He had rolled up his shirtsleeves above the elbows and was vigorously washing his hands and arms with Tiel's bottled cleanser. He then bathed them with vinegar. He passed the bottles to Tiel. "Use both liberally. But quickly."

"I don't want Ronnie watching," Sabra said.

"Sabra? Why not?"

"I mean it, Ronnie. Go away."

Doc spoke to him over his shoulder. "It might be best, Ronnie." Reluctantly the boy backed away.

In Cain's doctor's kit, Doc found a pair of gloves and pulled them on—expertly, Tiel noticed. He snapped them smartly around his wrists. "At least he did something right," he muttered. "There's a whole box of them. Get yourself a pair."

She had just managed to get the gloves on when Sabra had another contraction. "Don't bear down if you can keep from it," Doc instructed. "I don't want you to tear." He placed his right hand on the perineum for additional support to avoid tearing, while his left hand gently rested on the baby's head. "Come on, Sabra. Pant now. Thata girl. You might move behind her," he said to Tiel. "Angle her up. Support her lower back."

He coached Sabra through the pain, and when it was over, she relaxed against Tiel's support.

"Almost there, Sabra," Doc told her in a gentle voice. "You're doing fine. Great, in fact."

And Tiel could have said the same for him. One had to admire the calm, competent manner in which he was dealing with the frightened girl.

"Are you okay?"

Tiel had been staring at him with overt admiration, but she didn't realize he was addressing her until he glanced up. "Me? I'm fine."

"You're not going to faint or anything?"

"I don't think so." Then, because his composure was contagious, she said, "No. I won't faint."

Sabra cried out, jerked into a semi-sitting position, and grunted with the effort of expelling the baby. Tiel rubbed her lower back, wishing there was more she could do to relieve the girl's suffering.

"Is she all right?" The anxious father was ignored.

"Try not to push," Doc reminded the girl. "It'll come now without your applying additional pressure. Ride the pain. Good, good. The head's almost out."

The contraction abated and Sabra's body collapsed with fatigue. She was crying. "It hurts."

"I know." Doc spoke in a soothing voice, but unseen by Sabra, his face registered profound regret. She was bleeding profusely from tearing tissue. "You're doing fine, Sabra," he lied. "Soon you'll have your baby."

Very soon, as it turned out. After all the concern the child's slow progress had given them, in the final seconds it was eager to make its way into the world.

During the next contraction, almost before Tiel could assimilate the miracle she was witnessing, she watched the baby's head emerge facedown. Doc's hand guided it only a little before it instinctually turned sideways. When Tiel saw the newborn's face, its eyes wide open, she murmured, "Oh my God," and she meant it literally, like a prayer, because it was an awe-inspiring, almost spiritual phenomenon to behold.

But there the miracle stopped, because the baby's shoulders still could not clear the birth canal.

"What's happening?" Ronnie asked when Sabra screamed.

The telephone rang. Donna was nearest to it and she answered. "Hello?"

"I know it hurts, Sabra," Doc said. "The next two or three contractions should do it. Okay?"

"I can't," she sobbed. "I can't."

"This guy name o' Calloway wants to know who got shot," Donna informed them. No one paid any attention to her.

"Doing great, Sabra," Doc was saying. "Get ready. Pant." Glancing at Tiel, he said, "Be her coach."

Tiel began to pant along with Sabra as she watched Doc's hands moving around the baby's neck. Noticing her alarm, he said softly, "Just checking to make sure the cord wasn't wrapped around it."

"Is it okay?" Sabra asked through clenched teeth.

"So far it's a textbook birth."

Tiel heard Donna telling Calloway, "Nope, he ain't

dead, but he deserves to be and so does the damn fool that sent him in here." She then slammed down the receiver.

"Here we go, here we go. Your baby's here, Sabra." Sweat was running into Doc's eyebrows from his hairline, but he seemed unaware of it. "That's it. That's the way."

Her scream would haunt Tiel's dreams for many nights to come. More tissue was torn when the child's shoulders pushed through. A small incision under local anesthetic would have spared her that agony, but there was no help for it.

The only blessing to come of it was the wriggling baby that slipped into Doc's waiting hands. "It's a girl, Sabra. And she's a beauty. Ronnie, you have a baby daughter."

Donna, Vern, and Gladys cheered and applauded. Tiel sniffed back tears as she watched Doc tilt the infant's head down to help clear her breathing passages since they had no aspirator. Thankfully, she began crying immediately. A wide grin of relief split his austere face.

Tiel wasn't allowed to marvel for long because Doc was passing the infant to her. The newborn was so slippery she feared dropping her. But she managed to cradle her and get a towel around her. "Lay her on her mother's tummy." Tiel did as Doc instructed.

Sabra stared at her bawling newborn with wonderment and asked in a fearful whisper, "Is she all right?"

"Her lungs certainly seem to be," Tiel said, laughing. She ran a quick inventory. "All fingers and toes accounted for. Looks like her hair is going to be light like yours."

"Ronnie, can you see her?" Sabra called to him.

"Yeah." The boy was dividing his glance between her and the Mexicans, who seemed totally disenchanted by the wonders of birth. "She's beautiful. Well, I mean she will be when she's all cleaned up. How're you?"

"Perfect," Sabra replied.

But she wasn't. Blood had quickly saturated the pads beneath her. Doc tried to stanch it with sanitary napkins.

"Ask Gladys to bring me some more of those. I'm afraid we're going to need them."

Tiel summoned over Gladys and gave her the assignment. She was back in half a minute with another box of pads. "Did you get that man tied up?" Tiel asked.

"Vern's still working on him, but he won't be going anywhere anytime soon."

While Doc continued to work on Sabra, Tiel tried to distract her. "What are you going to name your daughter?"

Sabra was inspecting the infant with blatant adoration and unqualified love. "We decided on Katherine. I like the classic names."

"So do I. And I think Katherine is going to suit her."

Suddenly Sabra's face contorted with pain. "What's happening?"

"It's the placenta," Doc explained. "Where Katherine's been living the past nine months. Your uterus contracts to expel it just like it did to get Katherine on her way. It'll hurt a little, but nothing like having the baby. Once it's out, we'll clean you up and then let you rest. How does that sound?"

To Tiel he said, "Get one of those garbage sacks ready, please. I'll need to save this. It'll be examined later."

She did as asked and again distracted Sabra by talk-

ing about the baby. In a short time, Doc had the after-
birth wrapped up and out of sight, but still tethered to
the baby by the cord. Tiel wanted to ask why he hadn't
cut it yet, but he was busy.

A good five minutes later, he peeled off the bloody
gloves, picked up the blood-pressure cuff, and wrapped
it around Sabra's biceps. "How're you doing?"

"Good," she said, but her eye sockets were sunken
and shadowed. Her smile was wan. "How's Ronnie
holding up?"

"You should talk him into ending this, Sabra," Tiel
said gently.

"I can't. Now that I've got Katherine, I can't risk my
Daddy placing her up for adoption."

"He can't do that without your consent."

"He can do anything."

"What about your mother? Whose side is she on?"

"Daddy's, of course."

Doc read the gauge and released the cuff. "Try to get
some rest. I'm doing my best to keep your bleeding at
a minimum. I'll be asking a favor of you later on, so I'd
like you to take a nap now if you can."

"It hurts. Down there."

"I know. I'm sorry."

"It's not your fault," she said weakly. Her eyes began
to close. "You were super cool, Doc."

Tiel and Doc watched as her breathing became regular and her muscles relaxed. Tiel lifted Katherine off
her mother's chest. Sabra mumbled a protest but was
too exhausted to put up much resistance. "I'm only going to clean her up a little. When you wake up, you can
have her right back. Okay?"

Tiel took the girl's silence for permission to take the
infant away. "What about the cord?" she asked Doc.

"I've been waiting until it was safe."

The cord had stopped pulsing and was no longer ropy, but thinner and flatter. He tied it tightly in two places with shoestrings, leaving about an inch between them. Tiel turned her head aside when he cut it.

The placenta now completely free of the baby, Doc tightly sealed the trash bag and once again relied on Gladys's help, asking her to put the bag in the refrigerator before continuing to minister to the new mother.

Tiel opened the box of premoistened towelettes. "Do you think it's safe to use these on the baby?"

"I suppose. That's what they're for," Doc replied. Although Katherine put up little peeps of protest, Tiel sponged her with the wipes, which smelled pleasantly of baby powder. Having had no experience with newborns, she was nervous about the task. She also continued to monitor Sabra's gentle breathing.

"I applaud her courage," she remarked. "I also can't help but sympathize with them. From what I know of Russell Dendy, I'd have run away from him too."

"You know him?"

"Only through the media. I wonder if he was instrumental in sending Cain in here?"

"Why'd you hit him over the head?"

"Referring to my attack on a federal agent?" she asked, making a grim joke of it. "I was trying to prevent a disaster."

"I commend your swift action and only wish I'd thought of it."

"I had the advantage of standing behind him." She wrapped Katherine in a fresh towel and held her against her chest for warmth. "I suppose Agent Cain was only doing his duty. And it took a certain amount of bravery to walk into a situation like this. But I didn't want him to shoot Ronnie. And, just as earnestly, I didn't want Ronnie to shoot him. I acted on impulse."

"And weren't you just a little pissed to discover that Cain wasn't a doctor?"

She looked at him and smiled conspiratorially. "Don't tell."

"I promise."

"How'd you know he wasn't a medical man? What gave him away?"

"Sabra's vitals weren't his first concern. For instance, he didn't take her blood pressure. He didn't seem to grasp the seriousness of her condition, so I began to suspect him and tested his knowledge. When the cervix is dilated eight to ten centimeters, all systems are go. He flunked the test."

"We both might get sentenced to years of hard labor in federal prison."

"Better that than letting him shoot Ronnie."

"Amen to that." She glanced down at the infant, who was now sleeping. "How about the baby? Is she okay?"

"Let's take a look."

Tiel lay Katherine on her lap. Doc folded back the towel and examined the tiny newborn, who wasn't even as long as his forearm. His hands looked large and masculine against her baby pinkness, but their touch was tender, especially when he taped the tied-off cord to her tummy.

"She's small," he observed. "A couple weeks premature, I'd guess. She seems okay, though. Breathing all right. But she should be in a hospital neonatal unit. It's important that we keep her warm. Try and keep her head covered."

"All right."

He was leaning close to Tiel. Close enough for her

to distinguish each tiny line that radiated from the outer corners of his eyes. The irises of his eyes were grayish green, the lashes very black, several shades darker than his medium brown hair. His chin and jaw were showing stubble, which was attractive. Through the tear in his shirtsleeve, she noticed that blood had soaked through the makeshift bandage.

"Does your shoulder hurt?"

When he raised his head, they almost bumped noses. Their eyes were engaged for several seconds before he turned his head to check his shoulder wound. He looked at it as though he'd forgotten it was there. "No. It's fine." Hastily he added, "Better put one of those diapers on her, then wrap her up again."

Tiel ineptly diapered the baby while Doc checked on the new mother.

"Is all that blood..." Tiel purposefully left the question incomplete, afraid that Ronnie would overhear. Since Tiel had never witnessed a birth, she didn't know if the amount that Sabra had bled was normal or cause for alarm. To her, it appeared an inordinate amount, and if she was reading Doc right, he was concerned.

"Much more than there should be." He kept his voice low for the same reason she had. Draping the sheet over Sabra's thighs, he began massaging her abdomen. "Sometimes this helps curb the bleeding," he said in reply to Tiel's unspoken question.

"If it doesn't?"

"It can't go on for long before we've got real problems. I wish I could've done an episiotomy, saved her this."

"Don't blame yourself. Under the circumstances and given the conditions, you did amazingly well, Dr. Stanwick."

Chapter 7

It was out before she could recall it. She hadn't intended for Doc to know that she recognized him. Not yet, anyway.

Although maybe her slip of the tongue had been subconsciously intentional. Maybe she had addressed him by name just to see how he would react. Her reporter's yen for provoking a response to an unexpected question or statement had goaded her into tossing out his name to see what his spontaneous, unrehearsed, and therefore candid reaction would be.

His spontaneous, unrehearsed, and candid reaction was telling. In sequence he looked at first astonished, then mystified, then irked. Finally, it was as though a shutter had been slammed shut over his eyes.

Tiel held his stare, her steady gaze virtually daring him to deny that he was Dr. Bradley Stanwick. Or had been in his previous life.

The telephone rang again.

"Oh, hell," Donna grumbled. "What do I tell 'em this time?"

"Let me answer." Ronnie reached for the phone. "Mr. Calloway? No, like the lady told you, he's not dead."

Sabra had been roused by the ringing telephone. She asked to hold her baby. Tiel laid the infant in her arms. The new mother cooed over how sweet Katherine looked now, how good she smelled.

Tiel stood up and stretched. She hadn't realized until now how taxing the final hour of labor and the birth had been. Her fatigue couldn't compare to Sabra's, of course, but she was exhausted nonetheless.

Physically exhausted, but mentally charged. She took stock of the present situation. Gladys and Vern were sitting together quietly, holding hands. They looked tired but content, as though the night's events were being enacted for their entertainment.

Donna was hugging her bony chest with her skinny arms and picking at the loose, scaly sacks of skin that passed for elbows. The taller, leaner Mexican man was focused on Ronnie and the telephone. His friend was watching the FBI agent, who showed signs of coming around.

Vern had propped Agent Cain's back against the counter with his legs and feet stretched out in front of him. His ankles were bound together with silver duct tape. His wrists were likewise secured behind his back. His head was bowed low over his chest, but every now and then he tried to lift it, and when he did, he moaned.

"We've got him tied up," Ronnie was telling Calloway over the telephone. "We fired our guns almost at the same time, but the only one hit was Doc. No, he's okay." Ronnie glanced at Doc, who nodded in agreement. "Who's Ms. McCoy?"

"Me," Tiel said, stepping forward.

"How come?" Ronnie gave Tiel a quizzical once-over. "Well, I guess it's okay. How'd you know her name? Okay, hold on." As he extended the receiver to Tiel, he asked, "Are you famous or something?"

"Not so you'd notice." She took the receiver. "Hello?"

The voice was government-issue—crisp and concise. "Ms. McCoy, FBI Special Agent Bill Calloway."

"Hello."

"Are you in a position to speak freely?"

"Yes."

"You're under no duress?"

"No."

"What's the situation there?"

"Exactly as Ronnie described to you. Agent Cain caused a near disaster, but we were able to quell it."

Taken aback, the senior agent was slow to respond. "I beg your pardon?"

"Sending him in here was a bad call. Miss Dendy needed an obstetric specialist, not the cavalry."

"We didn't know—"

"Well now you do. This isn't Mount Carmel or Ruby Ridge. I'm not trying to tell you how to do your job—"

"Really?" he said dryly.

"But I urge you to cooperate with Mr. Davison from now on."

"It's the Bureau's policy not to negotiate with hostage-takers."

"These aren't terrorists," she exclaimed. "They're a couple of kids who are confused and scared and feel that they have exhausted all other options."

Raised voices could be heard in the background.

Calloway covered the mouthpiece to speak to someone else. Agent Cain raised his head and looked up at Tiel through bleary eyes. Did he recognize her as the one who had knocked his lights out with a can of chili?

"Mr. Dendy is very concerned about his daughter's welfare," Calloway said when he came back on the line. "The cashier—Donna?—told me that Sabra has delivered."

"A baby girl. Both are... stable." Tiel glanced at Doc, and he gave her a small nod. "Assure Mr. Dendy that his daughter is in no immediate danger."

"Sheriff Montez informs me there's a local man in there with you who has some medical training."

"That's right. He assisted Sabra through the labor and birth."

Doc's eyes narrowed a fraction—the gunslinger about to draw.

"Sheriff Montez can't recall his last name. Says he goes by Doc."

"Correct."

"You don't know his name?"

Tiel considered her options. She had been totally involved with the labor and delivery, but she wasn't entirely unaware of what had been happening outside. She'd heard the clap of helicopter rotors. Some would be police and medical choppers, but she would bet they also indicated the arrival of media from Dallas–Fort Worth, Austin, Houston. Big stations. Network affiliates.

The active role she was playing in this unfolding story had automatically elevated its media-worthiness. She wasn't what she would term famous, but, in all humility, she wasn't a nonentity, either. She was seen nearly every night on the evening news in her television market. Those newscasts were also aired on cable stations in smaller markets throughout Texas and into Oklahoma, which amounted to several million viewers. She was a flavor-enhancing ingredient to an already juicy story. Throw into that mix the involvement of Dr. Bradley Stanwick, who three years ago had disappeared from the public eye shrouded in scandal, and you had a tasty potboiler that would cause a feeding frenzy among the press corps.

But Tiel wanted it to be *her* potboiler.

If she gave away Doc's identity now, she could kiss her exclusive good-bye. Everyone else would report it first. The story would be broadcast before she had filed her initial report. By the time she could produce her own account of events, the resurfacing of Dr. Stanwick would be old news.

Gully would probably never forgive her for this decision, but, for the time being, she was going to keep this spicy tidbit as her secret ingredient.

So she avoided giving Calloway a direct answer. "Doc did an incredible job under very trying circumstances. Sabra responds to him favorably. She trusts him."

"I understand he was wounded during the exchange of gunfire."

"A scratch, nothing more. All of us are all right, Mr. Calloway," she said impatiently. "We're tired, but otherwise unharmed, and I can't emphasize that enough."

"You're not being forced to say this?"

"Absolutely not. The last thing Ronnie wants is for someone to get hurt."

"That's right," the boy said. "I just want to be able to walk out of here with Sabra and my baby, free to go our own way."

Tiel conveyed his wish to Calloway, who said, "Ms. McCoy, you know I can't let that happen."

"Allowances could be made."

"I don't have the authority to—"

"Mr. Calloway, are *you* in a position to speak freely?"
After a momentary pause, he said, "Go ahead."

"If you've had any interaction with Russell Dendy,
then you can well understand why these two young people felt desperate enough to do what they've done."

"I can't comment on that directly, but I understand
your meaning."

Apparently Dendy was within earshot. "By all accounts the man is a tyrant," Tiel continued. "I don't
know if you're aware of this, but he has pledged to
forcibly separate these two and put the baby up for
adoption. Ronnie and Sabra want only the liberty to de-
cide their own future and that of their child. This is a
family crisis, Mr. Calloway, and that's how it should be
handled. Perhaps Mr. Dendy would consent to a mediator who could help them work through their differences
and reach an agreement."

"Ronnie Davison still has a lot to answer for, Ms.
McCoy. Armed robbery, for starters."

"I'm sure Ronnie is willing to accept responsibility for
his actions."

"Let me talk to him." Ronnie took the receiver from
her. "Listen, Mr. Calloway, I'm not a criminal. Not until
today, that is. I've never even gotten a speeding ticket.
But I'm not going to let Mr. Dendy dictate my baby
girl's future. From where I stood, I couldn't see any
other way to get away from him."

"Tell him what we decided, Ronnie," Sabra called
out.

He looked down at her where she lay with the newborn cradled in her arms, and his face took on a pained
expression. "Talk to Sabra's dad, Mr. Calloway. Per-

suade him to leave us alone. Then I'll release everybody."

He listened for a moment, then said, "I know they
need to be in the hospital. The sooner the better. So
you've got one hour to get back to me." Another pause.
"Or what?" he said, obviously repeating Calloway's
question. Ronnie glanced again at Sabra. She clutched
her baby daughter tighter to her chest, and nodded. "I'll
tell you in an hour." He hung up abruptly.

Addressing his hostages, he said, "Okay, you all
heard. I don't want to hurt anybody. I want all of us to
walk out of here. So everybody just relax." He glanced
up at the wall clock. "Sixty minutes, it could be over."

"What if her old man don't agree to let y'all alone?"
Donna asked. "What're you gonna do to us?"

"Why don't you sit down and be quiet?" Vern said
querulously.

"Why don't you kiss my ass, old man?" she retorted.
"You're not the boss of me. I wanna know, am I gonna
live or die? An hour from now, is he gonna start popping
us?"

An uneasy silence descended over the group. All eyes
turned to Ronnie, but he stubbornly refused to acknowledge the unspoken question in their eyes.

Agent Cain had either lapsed into unconsciousness
again or was hanging his head in shame over his failure
to bring the standoff to an end. In any event, his chin
was resting on his chest.

Donna's elbows were subjected to more picking.

Vern and Gladys were showing signs of fatigue. Now
that the excitement of the birth was over, their liveliness
had waned. Gladys's head was resting on Vern's
shoulder.

Tiel crouched down beside Doc, who was attending

to Sabra again. Her eyes were closed. Baby Katherine was sleeping in her mother's arms. "How is she?"

"Too goddamn much bleeding, and her blood pressure's falling."

"What can you do?"

"I tried massaging the uterus, but rather than slowing the bleeding, it increased it." His brow was furrowed with consternation. "There is something else."

"What?"

"Nursing."

"Could she be lactating this soon?"

"No. Have you ever heard of oxytocin?"

"I assume it's a female thing."

"A hormone that helps eject breast milk. It also causes the uterus to contract, which reduces the bleeding. Sucking stimulates the release of the hormone."

"Oh. Then why haven't you—"

"Because I thought she might be on her way to a hospital by now. Besides, she's already had rather a lot to deal with."

They were quiet for a moment, both looking at Sabra and disliking her paleness. "I'm afraid of infection too," he said. "Dammit, they both need to be hospitalized. What's that Calloway like? Typical hard-ass?"

"All business, definitely. But he sounds reasonable. Dendy, on the other hand, is a raving maniac. I could hear him in the background issuing threats and ultimatums." She glanced at Ronnie, who was dividing his attention between the parking lot and the Mexican duo, who were becoming steadily and increasingly edgy. "He won't execute us, will he?"

Seemingly in no hurry to address her question, Doc finished replacing the pads beneath Sabra, then leaned against the freezer chest and raised one knee. Propping his elbow on it, he wearily raked a hand through his hair. By city standards, it could have stood a trim. But somehow, on him, in this environment, the unkempt look was fitting.

"I don't know what he'll do, Ms. McCoy. The misery that human beings are capable of inflicting on one another has never failed to fascinate and repel me. I don't think the boy has got it in him to line us up and shoot us, but there's no guarantee that he won't. In any event, talking about it won't affect the outcome."

"That's a rather fatalistic outlook."

"You asked." He shrugged indifferently. "We don't have to talk about it."

"Then what do you want to talk about?"

"Nothing."

"Bullshit," she said, wanting to surprise him and succeeding. "You want to know how I recognized you."

He merely looked at her, saying nothing. He'd built up quite an armor, but part of her job was piercing invisible armor.

"When I first saw you, I thought you looked familiar but couldn't place you. Then sometime during the birthing process, just before the delivery, it occurred to me who you were. I think the way you handled Sabra was the giveaway."

"You've got a remarkable memory, Ms. McCoy."

"Tiel. And my memory might be sharper than that of the average Jane Q. Public. You see, I covered your story." She recited the call letters of the television station for which she worked.

He muttered an expletive. "So you were among the hordes of reporters who made my life a living hell?"

"I'm good at my job."

He snuffled a deprecating laugh. "I'll bet you are."

He readjusted his long legs, but his eyes never left hers. "Do you like what you do?"

"Very much."

"You enjoy preying on people who are already down, exposing their hardship to public scrutiny, making it impossible for them to pick up the pieces of their already shattered lives?"

"You blame the media for your difficulties?"

"In large part, yeah."

"For instance?"

"For instance, the hospital buckled beneath the weight of bad publicity. Bad publicity generated and nurtured by people like you."

"You generated your own negative publicity, Dr. Stanwick."

Angrily, he turned his head away, and Tiel realized she had struck a chord.

Dr. Bradley Stanwick had been an oncologist of renown, practicing in one of the most progressive cancer-treatment centers in the world. Patients came from all over the globe, usually in a last-hope attempt to save themselves from dying. His clinic couldn't save them all, of course, but it had maintained an excellent track record of staving off the ravages of the disease and prolonging life, while also providing the patient a quality of life that made living longer worthwhile.

That's why it was such a cruel irony when Bradley Stanwick's young, beautiful, vivacious wife was stricken with inoperable pancreatic cancer.

Neither he nor his brilliant colleagues could retard its rapid spread. Within weeks of her diagnosis, she was confined to bed. She opted for aggressive chemotherapy and radiation, but the side effects were almost as lethal as the disease the treatments were intended to combat.

Her immune system weakened; she developed pneumonia. One by one her systems began to falter, then fail.

Not wishing her senses to be dulled by pain-relieving drugs, she declined them. However, during the last few days of her life, her suffering became so intense that she finally consented to a painkilling drug that she could self-administer through an IV.

All this Tiel learned through background research. Dr. and Mrs. Bradley didn't become news until after her death. Until she died, they were just a sad statistic, the victims of an insidious disease.

But following her funeral, disgruntled in-laws began to make noises that perhaps their son-in-law had accelerated his wife's passing. Specifically, he had enabled her to kill herself by setting the dosage on the self-administering mechanism so high that she actually had succumbed to a lethal amount of narcotics. They alleged that her sizeable inheritance was his enticement to speed things along.

From the start, Tiel had thought the allegations were nonsense. It was a foregone conclusion that Mrs. Bradley's life expectancy was a matter of days. A man due to inherit a fortune could afford to wait until nature took its course. Besides, Dr. Stanwick was affluent in his own right, although he put a lot of his income back into the oncology clinic to be used for research and indigent patient care.

Even if he had euthanized his wife, Tiel wasn't ready to cast the first stone. The controversy surrounding euthanasia left her in a moral quandary to which she had no satisfactory resolution. On that subject, she tended to agree with the last impassioned speaker.

But, strictly from a practical standpoint, she strongly doubted that Bradley Stanwick would risk his reputation even for his beloved wife's sake.

Unfortunately for him, his in-laws persisted until the DA's office ordered an investigation—which proved to be a waste of time and manpower. No evidence was found to substantiate the relatives' charge of criminal wrongdoing. There was no indication that Dr. Stanwick had done anything to hasten his wife's death. The DA declined even to present the case to the grand jury, claiming there was no basis for it whatsoever.

Nevertheless, the story didn't end there. During the weeks that investigators were interrogating Dr. Stanwick, his colleagues, his staff, friends, family, and former patients, every aspect of his life was extensively examined and debated. He lived beneath a shadow of suspicion that was especially unsettling since the majority of his patients were considered terminally, irreversibly ill.

The hospital where he practiced soon found itself in the spotlight too. Rather than standing behind him, the administrators voted unanimously to revoke his privileges at the facility until he was cleared of all suspicion. No fool, Bradley Stanwick knew he would never be cleared of *all* suspicion. Once a seed of doubt is planted in the public's mind, it usually finds fertile ground and flourishes.

Perhaps the ultimate betrayal came from his partners at the clinic he had established. After working together for years, pooling their research and case studies, combining their knowledge, skills, and theories, forging friendships as well as professional alliances, they asked him to resign.

He sold his share of the practice to his former partners, unloaded his stately home in Highland Park for a fraction of its appraised value, and, with a "Screw you all" attitude, left Dallas for parts unknown. That's where the story ended. If Tiel hadn't lost her way and wound up in Rojo Flats, she probably would never have thought of him again.

She asked him now, "Is Sabra the first patient you've treated since you left Dallas?"

"She isn't a patient, and I didn't treat her. I was a cancer doctor, not an OB-GYN. This is an emergency situation, and I responded. Just as you did. Just as everybody has."

"That's false modesty, Doc. None of us could have done for Sabra what you did."

"Ronnie, okay if I get a drink?" he suddenly called out to the boy.

"Sure. Okay. The others could probably use some water too."

Leaning forward, Doc took a six-pack of bottled water from the shelf. After taking two of the plastic bottles for Tiel and himself, he passed the rest up to the boy, who then asked Donna to distribute them.

He drank almost half his bottle in one swallow. Tiel twisted off the cap and drank from her bottle, sighing after taking a long draft. "Good idea. Trying to change the subject?"

"Good guess."

"You don't practice medicine here in Rojo Flats?"

"I told you. I ranch."

"But they know you around here as Doc."

"Everybody in a small town knows everything about everyone."

"But you must've told somebody. Otherwise, how'd it get around—"

"Look, Ms. McCoy—"

"Tiel."

"I don't know how it got around that I once practiced medicine. Even if I did, what's it to you?"

"Just curious."

"Uh-huh." He was looking straight ahead, away from her. "This isn't an interview. You won't get an interview from me. So why not save yourself the breath? You might need it later."

"Prior to the...the episode, you lived a very active life. Don't you miss being at the center of things?"

"No."

"You don't get bored out here?"

"No."

"Aren't you lonesome?"

"For what?"

"Companionship."

He turned his head and readjusted his position so that his shoulders and torso were almost facing her. "Sometimes." His eyes moved downward, over her. "You volunteering to help me out on that?"

"Oh, please."

And when she said that, he began to laugh, letting her know that he hadn't been serious.

She hated herself for falling for the ruse. "I hoped you were above that sexist crap."

Serious again, he said, "And I hoped you were above asking questions, particularly personal ones, at a time like this. Just as I was beginning to like you."

Strangely, the way he was looking at her now, with that probing intensity, had a greater effect than the smarmy sexual insinuation. That had been phony. This was real. Her tummy lifted weightlessly.

But then an uproar on the far side of the store brought her and Doc scrambling to their feet.

Chapter 8

Tiel had dubbed the shorter, stockier Mexican man Juan. It was he who had caused the commotion. He was bending over Agent Cain, lavishly cursing him—at least she assumed he was cursing. His shouted Spanish had an epithetical quality.

Cain was repeatedly screaming, "What the hell?" and futilely straining to free himself from the duct tape.

To everyone's dismay, Juan slapped a strip of duct tape over the FBI agent's mouth to shut him up. Meanwhile, Juan's taller companion let fly with a stream of Spanish that sounded both reproachful and confused by Juan's sudden attack on the agent.

Ronnie brandished his pistol, shouting, "What's going on? What're you doing there? Vern, what happened?"

"Damned if I know. I had sorta dozed off. I woke up when they started tussling and yelling at one another."

"He just jumped on him," Gladys contributed in her prissy manner. "For no apparent reason. I don't trust him. Or his friend either, for that matter."

"Que pasa?" Doc asked.

The others fell abruptly silent, surprised that he spoke Spanish. Apparently Juan was more surprised than anyone. He whipped his head around and glared at Doc. Undeterred by the smoldering eyes, Doc posed the question a second time.

"Nada," Juan muttered beneath his breath.

Then Doc just stood there and exchanged glowers with the Mexican. "Well?" Tiel prompted.

"Well, what? That's the extent of my Spanish vocabulary except for hello, good-bye, please, thank you, and shit. None apply to this particular situation."

"Why'd you jump him?" Ronnie asked the Mexican man. "What's the matter with you?"

Donna said, "He's a nutcase, that's what. Knew it the minute I laid eyes on him."

Juan answered in Spanish, but Ronnie impatiently shook his head. "I can't understand you. Just take that tape off his mouth. Do it!" he ordered when Juan failed to obey immediately. Ronnie made himself understood by pantomiming peeling the tape off Cain, who was listening and watching the proceedings with round, wide, fearful eyes.

The Mexican leaned down, pinched up a corner of the tape, and ripped it off the agent's lips. He yelped in pain, then shouted, "You son of a bitch!"

Juan actually seemed pleased with himself. He glanced at his partner and they both laughed, as though amused by the federal agent's embarrassment and discomfort.

"You're all going to jail. Every damn last one of you." Cain looked balefully at Tiel. "Especially you. You're to blame for the fix we're in."

"Me?"

"You impeded a federal officer and prevented him from performing his duty."

"I prevented you from needlessly taking a human life just so you could earn your spurs, or get your rocks off, or whatever it was that motivated you to come in here and further complicate an already complicated situation. Under the same set of circumstances I would clobber you again."

His hostile gaze moved from one hostage to the other, eventually landing on the Mexican who had attacked him. "I don't understand. What the hell is wrong with you people?" He nodded toward Ronnie. "He's the enemy, not me."

"We're only trying to keep this standoff from ending in disaster," Doc said.

"The only way that's going to happen is with a full surrender and the release of the hostages. It's a Bureau policy not to negotiate."

"We heard it already from Calloway," Tiel told him.

"If Calloway thinks I'm dead—"

"We assured him you aren't."

The agent sneered at Ronnie. "What makes you think he would believe you?"

"Because I confirmed it," Tiel said.

Doc, who'd returned his attention to Sabra, said, "I need another package of diapers."

They couldn't be for the baby, Tiel reasoned. Katherine hadn't wet that much. It took only a glance for her to understand that the replacements were for Sabra. Her bleeding had not abated. If anything it had increased.

"Ronnie, may I get another carton of diapers?"

"What's wrong? Something with the baby?"

"The baby's fine, but Sabra is bleeding."

"Oh Jesus."

"May I get the diapers?"

"Sure, sure," he said absently.

"Some hero you are, Davison," Cain remarked snidely. "To save your own skin, you're willing to let your girlfriend and baby die. Yeah, it takes real courage to let a woman bleed to death."

"Wish that Mex'can had used tape you cain't pull off," Donna grumbled. "You got a real fat mouth on you, G-man."

"For once, you're right, Donna," Gladys said. Speaking to Cain, she added, "What a hateful thing to say."

"All right, be quiet, all of you!" Ronnie said. Everyone instantly fell silent, except for the two Mexican men, who were conferring in whispers.

Tiel rushed back to Doc's side with the box of disposable diapers. She tore it open and unfolded a diaper for him, which he positioned beneath Sabra's hips. "What made you think of this?"

"She's bleeding through the napkins too fast. These diapers are lined with plastic."

The exchange was spoken in an undertone. Neither wanted to panic the girl or further fluster Ronnie, who was watching the wall clock behind the counter. Its long, sweeping second hand was circling dreadfully slowly.

Doc moved to Sabra's side and took her hand. "You're still bleeding a little heavier than I'd like."

Her eyes darted to Tiel, who laid a comforting hand on her shoulder. "No need for immediate alarm. Doc's just thinking ahead. He doesn't want things to get so bad they can't get better."

"That's right." Leaning down nearer to her, he spoke softly. "Would you please reconsider going to the hospital?"

"No!"

He appealed to her. "Before saying no, listen to me a minute. Please."

"Please, Sabra. Let Doc explain."

The girl's eyes moved back to Doc but they regarded him warily. "I'm thinking not only of you and the baby," he said, "but of Ronnie too. The sooner he brings this to an end, the better it's going to be for him."

"My daddy will kill him."

"No he won't. Not if you and Katherine are safe." Her eyes filled with tears. "You don't understand. He's only pretending to want us safe. Last night when we told him about the baby, he threatened to kill it. He said if he could, he would cut it out of me right then and strangle it with his bare hands. That's how much he hates Ronnie, how much he hates our being together."

Tiel gasped. She'd never heard a flattering word about Russell Dendy, but this testimony of his cruelty was shocking. How could anyone be so heartless? Doc's lips compressed into a thin line.

"That's the kind of person my daddy is," Sabra continued. "He hates to be crossed. He'll never forgive us for defying him. He'll have Ronnie sent to prison forever, and he'll make certain that I never see my baby again. I don't care what he does to me. If I can't be with them, it doesn't matter what happens to me."

She tilted her head down and rested her cheek against her newborn. The peach fuzz on the baby's small head blotted Sabra's tears from her cheeks. "You've both been great to me. Truly. I hate to disappoint you. But you won't change my mind about this. Until they let Ronnie and me walk out of here with Daddy's promise to leave us alone, I'm staying. Besides, Doc, I trust you more than I would any doctor at a hospital my daddy sent me to."

Doc swiped his sweating forehead with the back of his hand and sighed. He looked across at Tiel, who raised her shoulders in a defeatist's shrug.

"Okay," he said reluctantly. "I'll do my best."

"I don't doubt that." Sabra winced. "Is it really bad?"

"There's nothing I can do about the bleeding from the tear. But the vaginal bleeding...Remember earlier when I told you to rest because I might have to ask you to do something for me later?"

"Um-huh."

"Well, I'd like for you to nurse Katherine."

The girl shot Tiel a stunned glance. "The nursing will cause your uterus to contract and reduce the bleeding," she explained.

Doc smiled down at Sabra. "Ready to give it a try?"

"I guess so," she replied, although she seemed unsure and embarrassed.

"I'll help you." Tiel reached for the scissors, which had been wiped clean. "Why don't I use these to clip the shoulder seams of your dress? We can pin them back afterward, but that'll keep you from having to get undressed."

"That'd be good." She seemed relieved to give over some of the decision-making to Tiel.

"I'll let you ladies have some privacy. Uh, Ms., uh, Tiel?"

Doc motioned her to stand, and they held a brief, private consultation. "Do you know anything about this?"

"Nothing. My mother stopped breast-feeding me when I was three months old. I don't remember it."

He smiled wanly. "I meant other than being on the receiving end."

"I knew what you meant. That was a joke. But the answer is still no."

"Well then, of the three of you, Katherine will be the most knowledgeable. Position her correctly and she'll act on instinct. At least I hope she will. A few minutes on each breast."

"Right," Tiel said with a brisk nod.

She knelt down beside Sabra and applied the scissors to the shoulder seams of her sundress. "From now on, I suggest you start wearing tops that button up the front. Or something loose that you can lift up and drape over Katherine. One time, on a long flight to Los Angeles, I sat next to a mother with an infant. She breast-fed the baby all the way, and no one except me knew it, and I did only because she was in the seat beside me. She was completely covered the whole time."

The chatter was intentional, meant to distract Sabra and relieve her bashfulness. When she was finished ripping out the seams, Tiel peeled down one side of her bodice. "Now lower your bra strap and pull down the cup. Here, let me hold Katherine." Sabra looked around self-consciously. "No one can see," Tiel assured her.

"I know. But it feels weird."

"I'm sure it does."

When Sabra was ready, Tiel handed Katherine back to her. The newborn had been making soft, mewling noises, but the moment she felt the fullness of Sabra's breast against her cheek, her mouth began rooting for the nipple. She found it, tried to latch on, couldn't. After several attempts, the baby began to wail. She flailed tiny fists, and her face turned red.

"Everything okay?" Doc called.

"Fine," Tiel lied.

Sabra sobbed in frustration. "I'm not doing it right. What am I doing wrong?"

"Nothing, sweetheart, nothing," Tiel said soothingly.

"Katherine doesn't know how to be a baby any more than you know how to be a mom. You learn your roles together. That's what makes it so wonderful. But I've heard that a baby can sense the mother's frustration. The more relaxed you are, the easier it will be. Take a few deep breaths, then try again."

A second attempt was no more successful than the first. "Know what? I think it's your position," Tiel observed. "It's awkward for you and for her. Maybe if you could sit up."

"I can't. My bottom hurts too bad."

"What if Doc supported your back? It would relieve the pressure down there and enable you to cradle Katherine more comfortably."

"He'll see me," she protested in a tearful whisper.

"I'll fix it so he won't. Wait here. I'll be right back."

Earlier she had noticed a rack stocked with souvenir T-shirts. Before Ronnie could even ask what she was doing, she dashed to it and snatched one from the display. It was dusty, she noticed, but there was no help for that. Just as she was about to turn away, she yanked a second shirt from the rack.

By the time she returned with the T-shirts, Katherine was well into a wailing fit. Everyone else in the store was maintaining a respectful silence. Tiel spread one of the extra-large T-shirts over mother and baby. "There. He won't be able to see a thing. All right?"

"All right."

"Doc?"

He was there in a blink. "Yeah?"

"Could you please get behind Sabra and support her back, like I did during the birth?"

"Sure."

He knelt down behind the girl and helped ease her

into a semi-sitting position. "Now, just lean back against my chest. Come on, relax, Sabra. There. Comfortable?"

"Yes, I'm okay. Thanks."

Tiel raised a corner of the T-shirt just enough to peer beneath it. Katherine had stopped crying and was once again on her instinctive search. "Help her, Sabra," Tiel instructed softly. Sabra acted on instinct too. With only a little maneuvering and finessing, a tight suction was formed between breast and baby, and she began to suck vigorously.

Sabra laughed with delight. As did Tiel. She dropped the corner of the shirt and smiled at Doc.

"I assume everything is okay."

"They're pros." Tiel's bragging brought a wide smile to Sabra's chalky lips. Tiel asked, "Had you decided ahead of time to breast-feed?"

"Truthfully, I hadn't really thought about it. I was so preoccupied with worry that somebody was going to find out about the pregnancy, I didn't have much time to think about anything else."

"You can try it, then if it doesn't work out, you can switch to bottles. There's no shame in bottle-feeding."

"But I hear that nursing is better for the baby."

"That's what I hear too."

"You don't have kids?"

"No."

"Are you married?"

It seemed that Sabra had forgotten Doc was there. Her back was to him, so to her he was like a piece of furniture. Tiel, however, was facing him and keenly aware that he was listening to every word. "No. Single."

"Have you ever been?"

After a slight hesitation, she replied, "Years ago. For a short time."

"What happened?"

The grayish green eyes didn't waver. "We, uh, went different directions."

"Oh. Too bad."

"Yes, it was."

"How old were you?"

"Young."

"How old are you now?"

Tiel laughed nervously. "Older. Thirty-three last month."

"You'd better hurry up and find someone else. If you want to have a family, I mean."

"You sound like my mother."

"Do you?"

"Do I what?"

"Want to have another husband and kids?"

"Someday. Maybe. I've been awfully busy establishing my career."

"You could be a single mom."

"I've considered it, but I'm not sure I'd want that for my child. The jury's still out."

"I can't imagine not wanting a family," the girl said with a gentle smile for Katherine. "That's all Ronnie and I talk about. We want to have a big house out in the country. With lots of kids. I'm an only child. He has one little stepbrother, and they're twelve years apart in age. We want a large family."

"That's an admirable ambition."

Unobtrusively, Doc signaled Tiel with his chin that it was time to switch sides. Teil assisted Sabra, and soon Katherine was happily sucking away at the other breast.

Then the girl surprised them by angling her head back and asking, "What about you, Doc?"

"What about me?"

"Are you married?"

"My wife died three years ago."

Sabra's face fell. "Oh, I'm so sorry."

"Thank you."

"How'd she die? If you don't mind me asking."

He told her about his wife's illness, making no mention of the conflict that followed her demise.

"Any kids?"

"Unfortunately no. We had just begun talking about starting our family when she got sick. Like Ms. McCoy, she had a career. She was a microbiologist."

"Wow, she must've been smart."

"Brilliant, in fact." He smiled, although Sabra couldn't see it. "Much smarter than me."

"You must've loved each other a whole lot."

His smile gradually faded. What Sabra couldn't guess, but Tiel knew, was that his marriage hadn't been flawless and trouble-free. During the investigation into the circumstances surrounding Shari Stanwick's death, it was disclosed that she had engaged in an extramarital affair. Bradley Stanwick knew of his wife's unfaithfulness and generously assumed his share of the blame. His work schedule was demanding and often kept him out late and away from home.

But the two had loved each other and were committed to making the marriage work. They were in counseling and planning to stay together when her malignancy was diagnosed. Her illness had actually brought them closer together. At least that's what he had claimed to his accusers.

Tiel could see that, even after all this time, reminders of his wife's adultery still pained him.

When he became aware that Tiel was watching him, the wistfulness in his expression vanished. "That's enough for now," he said, speaking more brusquely than he probably intended.

"She's stopped sucking anyway," Sabra said. "I think she's gone to sleep."

While Sabra was readjusting her clothing, Tiel took the baby and changed her. Doc eased the girl back into her original position, then checked the diaper he'd placed beneath her. "Better. Thank God."

Tiel cuddled the baby close and planted a soft kiss on the top of her head before returning her to her mother's arms.

The telephone rang. The hour was up.

Everybody snapped to attention. Anticipated for an hour, the ringing telephone was jarring, because it represented the course of their future. Now that it was imminent, all seemed loathe to hear Calloway's response to Ronnie's demand. Especially Ronnie, who appeared more nervous even than before.

He looked over at Sabra and tried to smile, but his lips couldn't hold the expression for long. "Are you sure, Sabra?"

"Yes, Ronnie." She spoke quietly but with resolve and dignity. "Absolutely sure."

The boy wiped his hand on his pants leg before lifting the receiver off the hook. "Mr. Calloway?" Then, after a momentary pause, he exclaimed, *"Dad!"*

Chapter 9

Who's this?"

When the latest arrival was escorted into the FBI van, Calloway had ignored Russell Dendy's rude question and instead stood up to shake the man's hand. "Mr. Davison?"

"You've got to be kidding me." Dendy had sneered with disgust. "Who invited him?"

Calloway had pretended Dendy wasn't even there. "I'm Special Agent Bill Calloway."

"Cole Davison. Wish I could say it's a pleasure to meet you, Mr. Calloway."

Judging by his appearance, one would guess Davison to be a rancher. He wore faded Levi's and cowboy boots. His starched white shirt had pearl snaps in lieu of buttons. Upon entering the van, he'd politely removed a straw cowboy hat that had left a deep indentation in his hair and a pink stripe across his forehead, which was several shades paler than the lower two-thirds of his sun-tanned face. He had a stocky build and walked with a bowlegged gait.

He didn't ranch. He owned five fast-food franchises and lived in Hera only to escape "metropolises" like Tulia and Floydada.

Calloway had welcomed him with a "Thank you for coming so quickly, Mr. Davison."

"I'd've come whether you asked me to or not. Soon's I heard my boy was holed up here, I was anxious to get here. I was on my way out the door when you called."

Dendy, who'd been fuming in the background, had grabbed Davison by the shoulder and spun him around. He thrust his index finger into the other man's face. "It's your fault my daughter is in the mess she's in. If anything happens to her, you're dead and so is the miscreant you spawned—"

"Mr. Dendy," Calloway had interrupted sternly. "Once again I'm on the verge of having you physically removed from this van. One more word and you're out of here."

The millionaire, ignoring Calloway's warning, had continued his harangue. "Your kid," he'd declared, "seduced my daughter, got her pregnant, and then kidnaped her. I'm going to make it my life's mission that he never sees the light of day or breathes a breath of freedom. I'm going to make certain that he spends every single second of his miserable life in prison."

To Davison's credit, he had kept his cool. "It appears to me you're partly to blame for all this, Mr. Dendy. If you hadn't come down so hard on those kids they wouldn't've felt the need to run away. You know's well as I do that Ronnie didn't take your girl against her will. They love each other and ran away from you and your threats, is what I think."

"I don't give a fuck what you think."

"Well, I do," Calloway had said, shouting over Russell Dendy. "I want to hear Mr. Davison's take on the situation."

"You can call me Cole."

"All right, Cole. What do you know about this? Anything you can tell us about your son and his frame of mind will be helpful."

To which Dendy had said, "How about some sharpshooters? A SWAT team? Now *that* would be helpful."

"Using force would risk the lives of your daughter and her baby."

"Baby?" Davison had exclaimed. "It's come?"

"From what we understand she delivered a baby girl about two hours ago," Calloway had informed him. "Both are reportedly doing okay."

"Reportedly," Dendy had snorted. "For all I know my daughter is dead."

"She's not dead. Not according to Ms. McCoy."

"She could've been talking to save her own hide. That lunatic could have been holding a gun to her head!"

"I don't think so, Mr. Dendy," Calloway had said, striving to remain calm. "And neither does our psychologist, who was listening to my conversation with Ms. McCoy. She sounds in perfect control, not like someone under duress."

"Who's this Ms. McCoy?" Davison had wanted to know.

Calloway explained, then he'd regarded Davison closely. "When was the last time you spoke to Ronnie?"

"Last night. He and Sabra were about to go over to the Dendys' house and tell her parents about the baby."

"How long have you known about the pregnancy?"

"A few weeks."

Dendy's face had turned beet red. "And you didn't see fit to tell me?"

"No, sir, I didn't. My son confided in me. I couldn't betray his trust, although I urged him to tell you." He had turned his back on Dendy and addressed the remainder of his remarks to Calloway.

"I had to run up to Midkiff today on account of a deep fryer going out. I didn't get home until late this evening. Found a note from Ronnie on my kitchen table. It said they'd come by hoping to catch me. Said they had run away together and were headed for Mexico. Said they'd let me know how to reach them when they got where they were going."

"I'm surprised they would pay you a visit. Weren't they afraid you'd try and talk them into returning home?"

"Truth is, Mr. Calloway, I told Ronnie if they ever needed my help, I was pleased to offer it."

Dendy had attacked so quickly no one saw it coming, least of all Davison. Dendy landed on Davison's back with all his weight behind him. Davison would have fallen forward, had not Calloway caught him and broken his fall. As it was, both men landed hard against the wall of the van that was lined with computer terminals, TV monitors, video recorders, and surveillance equipment. Sheriff Montez grabbed Dendy by the shirt collar and hauled him backward, slamming him into the opposite wall.

Calloway had instructed one of his subordinates to drag Dendy the hell out of there.

"No!" Dendy had had the wind knocked out of him and was gasping for breath, but he managed to rasp, "I want to hear what he has to say. Please."

Somewhat mollified, Calloway had relented. "There

will be no more of that crap, Dendy. Do you understand me?"

Dendy was red-faced and furious, but he nodded. "Yeah. I'll get even with this son of a bitch later. But I want to know what's going on."

Order restored, Calloway had asked Davison if he was all right. Davison had picked his cowboy hat off the floor and dusted it off on the leg of his jeans. "Never mind about me. I'm worried about those kids. The baby, too."

"Do you think Ronnie was coming to you for money?"

"Could be. Regardless of what Mr. Dendy here thinks, I didn't offer to help them run away. In fact, just the opposite. My advice to them was that they should stand up to him." The two parents exchanged dirty looks. "Anyhow," Davison had continued, "I reckon they could've used some cash. Ronnie works after school at a driving range to earn spending money, but his salary wouldn't finance a move to Mexico. Since I missed him today, I guess he decided to do this."

He'd gestured toward the store, his expression remorseful. "My boy's not a thief. His mother and stepfather have done a good job with him. He's a good boy. I reckon he was feeling desperate to take care of Sabra and the baby."

"He's taken care of her, all right. He's ruined her life."

Paying no attention to Dendy, Davison had asked Calloway, "So what's the plan? Have you got a plan?"

Calloway had brought Ronnie Davison's father up to speed. Checking his wristwatch, he'd added, "Fifty-seven minutes ago, he gave us an hour to persuade Mr.

Dendy to leave them alone. They want his word that he won't interfere in their lives, that he won't give away their baby. That—"

"Give away the baby?" Davison had looked at Dendy with patent dismay. "You threatened to give away their baby?" His disdainful expression spoke volumes. Shaking his head sadly, he'd turned back to Calloway. "What can I do?"

"Understand, Mr. Davison, that Ronnie will face criminal charges."

"I reckon he knows that."

"But the sooner he releases those hostages and surrenders, the better off he's going to be. So far no one's been hurt. Not seriously anyway. I'd like to keep it that way, for Ronnie's sake, as well as the others'."

"He won't be hurt?"

"You have my word on that."

"Tell me what to do."

That conversation had resulted in Cole Davison placing a call to the store just as the deadline expired.

"Dad!" Ronnie exclaimed. "Where're you calling from?"

Tiel and Doc moved forward and listened carefully to what Ronnie was saying into the telephone. Judging by his reaction, he hadn't expected the call to be from his father.

From what Gully had told her earlier, Tiel knew the two were close. She imagined Ronnie was feeling a mix of shame and embarrassment, as any child experiences when caught red-handed doing something wrong by a parent he respects. Perhaps Mr. Davison could impress upon his son the trouble he was in and influence him to end the standoff.

"No, Dad, Sabra's doing okay. You know how I feel

about her. I wouldn't've done anything to hurt her. Yeah, I know she should be in a hospital, but—"

"Tell him I'm not leaving you," Sabra called to him.

"It's not just me, Dad. Sabra says she won't go." As he listened, his eyes cut to Sabra and the baby. "She seems to be doing okay too. Ms. McCoy and Doc have been taking care of them. Yeah, I know it's serious."

The young man's features were taut with concentration. Tiel looked around at her fellow hostages. All, including the Mexican men, who didn't even understand the language, were still, silent, and alert.

Doc felt her gaze when it moved to him. He raised his shoulders in a small shrug, then returned his attention to Ronnie, who was gripping the receiver so tightly his knuckles had turned white. His forehead was beaded with sweat. His fingers nervously flexed and contracted around the pistol grip.

"Mr. Calloway seems like a decent man to me too, Dad. But it doesn't really matter what he says or guarantees. It's not the authorities we're running from. It's Mr. Dendy. We aren't going to give up our baby and have strangers adopt her. Yes he would!" the boy stressed in a voice that cracked with emotion. "He *would*."

"They don't know him," Sabra said, her voice as ragged as Ronnie's.

"Dad, I love you," Ronnie said into the receiver. "And I'm sorry if I've made you ashamed of me. But I can't give up. Not until Mr. Dendy promises to let Sabra keep the baby."

Whatever Ronnie was hearing made him shake his head and smile at Sabra sadly. "Then there's something you, Mr. Dendy, the FBI, and everybody else ought to know, Dad. We—Sabra and I—made a pact before we left Fort Worth."

Tiel's chest constricted. "Oh, no."

"We don't want to live apart. I think you know what that means, Dad. If Mr. Dendy won't give up his control of our lives, our future, we don't want a future."

"Ah, Jesus." Doc dragged his hand down his face.

"Yes, Dad, I do," the boy insisted. He was looking at Sabra, who nodded her head solemnly. "We won't live without each other. You tell that to Mr. Dendy and Mr. Calloway. If they don't let us leave and go our own way, nobody leaves here alive."

He hung up quickly. No one moved or said anything for several moments. Then, as though on cue, everyone began talking at once. Donna started to wail. Agent Cain kept up a litany of "You'll never get away with this." Vern professed his love for Gladys, while she begged Ronnie to think about his baby.

It was her statement that Ronnie addressed. "My dad will take Katherine and raise her like his own. He won't let Mr. Dendy get his hands on her."

"We decided all this ahead of time," Sabra said. "Last night."

"You can't mean it," Tiel said to her. "You can't."

"We do. It's the only way they'll understand how we feel about each other."

Tiel knelt down beside her. "Sabra, suicide isn't a viable way to make a point or win an argument. Think of your baby. She would never know you. Or Ronnie."

"She would never know us anyway. Not if my daddy had his way."

Tiel stood up and moved to stand beside Doc, who was making similarly urgent appeals to Ronnie. "To take that many lives, Sabra's life, you'd only be validating Dendy's low opinion of you. You've got to play smarter than him, Ronnie."

"No," the boy said stubbornly.

"Is that the legacy you want to leave your daughter?"

"We've thought about this for a long time," Ronnie said. "We gave Mr. Dendy an opportunity to accept us, and he refused. This is the only way out for us. I meant what I said. Sabra and I would rather die—"

"I don't think they're convinced."

"Huh?" He looked at Tiel, who had interrupted him. Doc also turned to her, equally surprised by her statement.

"I bet they think you're bluffing."

An idea had first occurred to her earlier, when Ronnie was trying to convince Calloway that all the hostages were safe, including Agent Cain. She'd temporarily shelved the notion while assisting Sabra with the breast-feeding. Now it took another foothold in her mind and was expanding even as she vocalized it.

"For them to feel the impact of your decision, they need to understand how serious you are."

"I've told them," Ronnie said.

"But seeing is believing."

"What are you suggesting?" This from Doc.

"There's media out there. I'm sure a camera crew from my station is among them. Let's get a cameraman in here to record you." The boy was listening. She drove home her point. "We see how earnest you are," she said, indicating the others. "But it's impossible to convey your sincerity over the telephone. If Calloway could see you when you speak, see that Sabra is in total agreement, then I think he, your father, and Mr. Dendy would give more credence to what you're saying."

"You mean I'd be on TV?" Donna asked, sounding pleased at the prospect.

Ronnie's lower lip was getting brutalized by his upper teeth. "Sabra, what do you think?"

"I don't know," she said with uncertainty.

"Another thing," Tiel argued, "if Mr. Dendy could see his granddaughter, he might back down altogether. You claim to be more afraid of him than you are of the FBI."

"We are. He's a lot more ruthless."

"But he's a human being. Video pictures of Katherine would be powerfully persuasive. Up till now she's been just 'the baby,' a symbol of your rebellion against him. A video would make her real to him, cause him to rethink his position. And with your father and Agent Calloway working on him, I believe he would weaken and capitulate."

"Agent Calloway is not going to compromise on the Bureau's policy." Cain might just as well have saved his breath because no one heeded him or his comment.

"What do you say?" Tiel asked. "Isn't it worth a try? You don't want to kill us, Ronnie. And you don't want to kill Sabra and yourself, either. Suicide is a permanent solution to a temporary problem."

"I'm not just blowing smoke!"

Tiel pounced on his emotional outburst. "Good! That's exactly what they need to see and hear. Use the videotape to convince them that you do not intend to back down."

He was struggling with indecision. "Sabra, what do you think?"

"Maybe we should, Ronnie." She glanced down at the child sleeping in her arms. "What Doc said about the legacy we leave Katherine...If there's another way out of this, isn't it worth a try at least?"

Tiel held her breath. She was near enough to Doc to tell that he was as taut as a piano wire.

"Okay," Ronnie said tersely. "One guy can come in.

And you'd better tell them not to pull any tricks like they did with him," he said, gesturing toward Cain.

Tiel exhaled shakily. "Even if they tried, I wouldn't let them. If a crew from my station isn't here yet, we'll wait for one. Unless I recognize the videographer, he doesn't come in, okay? I give you my word." She turned to Cain. "How can I contact Calloway?"

"I don't—"

"Don't give me any bullshit. What's the number?"

Chapter 10

⟫⟫◉⟪⟪

Tiel was washing her chest with one of the baby wipes when she sensed movement behind her. She glanced around quickly, and it would be difficult to say who was the most discomfited, her or Doc. His eyes involuntarily dropped to her lilac lace brassiere. Tiel felt a warm blush rise out of it.

"Sorry," he mumbled.

"I was a mess," she explained, bringing her shoulder back around to conceal her front. Her blouse had been stiff with the dried sanguineous fluid it had absorbed when she first held the newborn against her chest. Doc had been conferring with Ronnie, so Tiel had taken advantage of a moment's privacy to remove her blouse and wash. He'd returned before she expected him. "I thought I should clean up before appearing on camera."

She disposed of the towelette and picked up the spare T-shirt she had taken from the rack earlier. After pulling it on, she turned and held her arms out to her sides. On the front of the T-shirt was the Texas state flag with the word HOME underneath. "Not exactly haute couture," she remarked ruefully.

"It is in these parts." He checked on Sabra, then joined Tiel where she had sat down with her back to the freezer chest. She passed him a bottle of water. He drank after her with no compunction.

"How is she? Any better?"

Doc nodded a hesitant affirmative, but his brow was furrowed with concern. "She's lost a lot of blood. It's co-agulated somewhat, but she needs to be sutured."

"There wasn't a suture kit in the doctor's bag?" He shook his head. "I checked. So, even though the bleed-ing has slackened, infection is a real concern."

Sabra and the baby were sleeping. After Tiel's tele-phone conversation with Agent Calloway to arrange the videotaping, Ronnie had resumed his post. He was most wary of the Mexicans and Cain. He watched them vigi-lantly. Vern and Gladys were dozing, their heads together. Donna was thumbing through a tabloid magazine, much as she would do on any other night when business was slow. For the time being, everything was quiet.

"What about the baby?" Tiel asked Doc.

"Holding her own." He had listened to Katherine's chest through the stethoscope included in the doctor's kit. "Heartbeat's strong. Lungs sound okay. But I'll feel a lot better when she's getting neonatal care from ex-perts."

"Maybe it won't be much longer. My friend Gully runs our news operation. For several hours now he's known that I'm among the hostages. I'm almost certain our station has a crew already here. Calloway's checking on that, and promised to get back to me as soon as possi-ble. I have every confidence in the effectiveness of video. It will soon be over."

"I hope so," he said, giving the young mother and baby another worried glance.

"You did a terrific job, Doc." He looked at her suspiciously, as though waiting for the other shoe to drop. "I mean that sincerely. You're very good. Maybe you should have chosen obstetrics or pediatrics over oncology."

"Maybe I should have," he said grimly. "I didn't have a very good success rate combating cancer."

"You had an excellent success rate. Far above the average."

"Yeah, well..."

Yeah, well, I couldn't cure the one that really counted. My own wife. Tiel mentally finished the thought for him. It would be pointless to argue how commendable his efforts to conquer the disease had been when, in his own mind, that single casualty had cost him the war.

"What directed you toward oncology?"

At first it seemed he wasn't going to answer. Finally he said, "My kid brother died of lymphoma when he was nine."

"I'm sorry."

"It was a long time ago."

"How old were you?"

"Twelve, thirteen."

"But his death had a lasting impact on you."

"I remember how tough it was on my parents."

So he'd lost two people he loved to an enemy he had failed to defeat, Tiel thought. "You were powerless to save your brother or your wife," she observed aloud. "Is that why you quit?"

"You were there," he said curtly. "You know why I quit."

"I know only what you were willing to impart to journalists, which was precious little."

"It still is precious little."

"You were bitter."

"I was pissed." He raised his voice to the level of a stage whisper, but it was loud enough to cause Katherine to flinch in her mother's arms.

"At whom were you pissed?" She knew she was pressing her luck. If she probed too hard, too fast, he might clam up altogether. But she was willing to take the chance. "Were you angry at your in-laws for making an unfounded allegation? Or at your associates for withdrawing their support?"

"I was angry at everybody. At everything. Goddamn cancer. My own inadequacy."

"So you just threw in the towel."

"That's right, thinking 'What's the fucking use?' "

"I see, so you banished yourself to this no-man's-land where you could *really* be useful."

Her sarcasm wasn't lost on him. His features tightened with mounting annoyance. "Look, I don't need you or anybody else analyzing my decision. Or questioning it. Or judging it. If I decided to become a rancher, or a ballet dancer, or a bum, it's no one else's business."

"You're right. It's not."

"And while we're on the topic of business," he added in the same biting tone, "this videotape idea of yours..."

"What about it?"

"Is it strictly for Ronnie and Sabra's benefit?"

"Of course."

He looked at her with blatant mistrust, which stung. He even chuckled skeptically.

"I think anything we can do to sway Dendy will help defuse this situation." Even to her own ears she sounded self-defensive, but she continued anyway. "I don't get the impression that Agent Calloway is enjoying this standoff. Regardless of what Cain says, Calloway sounds like a decent man who's doing his job but doesn't relish the thought of blazing guns and bloodshed. I think he's willing to try and negotiate a peaceful settlement. I merely offered my services, which I believe will facilitate a peaceful resolution."

"But it'll also make one hell of a story for you."

His soft and intuitive voice, along with his piercing eyes, made her guiltily aware of the audio recorder in her pants pocket. "Okay, yes," she admitted uneasily, "it'll make a great story. But I'm personally involved with these kids. I helped bring their child into the world, so my idea isn't completely selfish.

"You're biased, Doc. You dislike reporters in general, and, given your experience with the media, your aversion is understandable. But I'm not as cold-hearted and unfeeling as you obviously think. I care a great deal what happens to Ronnie and Sabra and Katherine. I care what happens to all of us."

After a significant pause, he said quietly, "I believe that."

His eyes were just as piercing as before, but the substance of this gaze was different. The heat of vexation that had suffused her gradually intensified into heat of another kind.

"You were terrific, you know," he said. "With Sabra. You could've fallen apart on me. Freaked out. Thrown up. Fainted. Something. Instead you were a calming influence. A real help. Thanks."

"You're welcome." She laughed softly. "I was awfully nervous."

"So was I."

"No! Honestly?"

He drew an invisible *X* over his heart.

"You'd never know it."

"Well, I was. I haven't had that much experience with childbirth. I observed a few during med school. Assisted with a couple when I was a resident, but always in a well-equipped, sterile hospital with other doctors and nurses around. I'd forgot most of what I'd learned. This was a scary experience for me."

She stared into near space for a moment before her eyes came back to his. "I was nervous up to the point where I saw the baby crowning. Then the wonder of it all overtook me. It was...tremendous." The word fell short of defining the memorable experience, but she wasn't sure a single word could encompass it or capture its myriad dimensions. "Truly, Doc. Tremendous."

"I know what you mean."

Then for what seemed an endless time, they held each other's stare.

Finally he said, "If I ever find myself in another emergency childbirth situation..."

"You know who to call for backup. Partner."

She stuck out her hand, and he took it. But he didn't shake it to confirm the partnership. He held it. Not so tightly that it was uncomfortable, but snugly enough to make it personal, almost intimate.

Except for the time she had taped the gauze to his shoulder wound—and that had been so fleeting it really didn't count—this was the first time they had touched. The skin-to-skin connection was electric. It created a tingle that made Tiel want to pull her hand back quickly. Or to continue holding on to his forever.

"Do me one favor?" he asked softly.

Mutely, she nodded. "I don't want to be on camera."

Reluctantly she pulled her hand away. "But you're integral to the story."

"You said the story was secondary to your purpose."

"I also conceded that it's a heck of a story."

"I don't want to be on camera," he repeated. "Keep me out of it."

"I'm sorry, Doc, I can't. You're already in it. You're neck-deep in this story."

"For us in here I am. I had no choice but to get involved. But I don't owe anybody out there a damn thing, especially entertainment at the expense of my privacy. Agreed?"

"I'll see what I can do." The secreted tape recorder felt very heavy in the pocket of her slacks. "I can't speak for the cameraman."

He gave her a retiring look that asked her not to insult his intelligence. "Of course you can. You're calling the shots. Keep me out of it." He emphasized each word, so that there would be no misinterpretation of his meaning.

He got up to check on Sabra. As he moved away from her, Tiel wondered if his compliments and hand holding had been calculated to break down her defenses, a handsome man's way of buttering her up. Rather than taking a belligerent stance, had he purposefully shown her his softer side? The honey over vinegar approach, so to speak.

She also wondered what he would do when he learned that the tape about to be recorded wouldn't be the only source of video available to her when she put her story together. He had already been recorded on video and didn't know it.

She would have to worry about that later, though. The telephone was ringing.

Calloway quickly came to his feet when the van's side door opened. Sheriff Montez, whom Calloway had come to respect as a wise, savvy, and intuitive lawman, entered first. He motioned inside a bandy-legged, pot-bellied, balding man who smelled like the pack of Camels that were visible in the breast pocket of his shirt.

"My name's Gully."

"Special Agent Calloway." As they shook hands, he added, "Maybe we should talk outside. It's becoming crowded in here."

Inside the van now were three FBI agents in addition to Calloway, the FBI psychological profiler, Russell Dendy, Cole Davison, Sheriff Montez, and the new-comer, who said, "Then kick somebody else out, be-cause I'm staying until Tiel is safe and sound."

"You're the news assignments editor, is that correct?"

"Going on half a century. And tonight I left my news-room in the hands of a wet-behind-the-ears rookie with bleached hair and three silver hoops in his eyebrow, a smart-ass fresh out of UT with a degree in television." He snorted with derision at the presumption that broad-cast journalism was something that could be learned at college.

"I rarely leave my post, Mr. Calloway. And never in the hands of incompetents. That I did so tonight should give you some indication of how much I think of Tiel McCoy. So, no, sir, Mr. Calloway, my ass is a perma-nent fixture of this van until this business is over. You're Dendy, right?" Suddenly he turned to the Fort Worth millionaire.

Dendy didn't deign to reply to so brusque a greeting.

"Just so you know," Gully told him, "if anything happens to Tiel, I'm gonna rip out your goddamn guts. My opinion, you're the cause of all this." Leaving Dendy to smolder in his wrath, Gully turned back to Calloway. "Now, what is it Tiel's after? Whatever it is, she gets."

"I've consented to her request of sending in a video cameraman."

"He's outside, geared up and raring to go."

"First, I need to lay down a few ground rules for this recording."

Gully's eyes narrowed suspiciously. "Such as?"

"This tape must serve our purposes too."

Cole Davison stepped forward. "What purposes?"

"I want a view of the store's interior."

"What for?"

"This is a standoff, Mr. Davison. Hostages are being held at gunpoint. I need to know what's going on in there so I can respond accordingly."

"You promised me my son would not be hurt."

"He won't be. Nor will anyone else. Not if I can help it."

"Might freak out the boy if he thinks you're concentrating on the lay of the land instead of his message," Gully remarked.

"I want to know who is where inside that store." Calloway spoke with authority, quelling any further discussion on the matter. He didn't care who disliked it; that was a non-negotiable condition.

"That it?" Gully asked impatiently.

"That's it. I'll call Ms. McCoy now."

Gully motioned Calloway toward the telephone. "Get after it. If you're waiting on me, you're backing up."

Under other circumstances, Calloway would have laughed at the man's brazenness. But his voice was all business when he got through to Ronnie. "This is Agent Calloway. Let me speak to Ms. McCoy."

"Are you going to let us do the video?"

"That's what I need to talk to her about. Put her on, please." Within a second, the newswoman was on the line.

"Ms. McCoy, your cameraman..."

"Kip," Gully supplied.

"Kip is standing by."

"Thank you, Mr. Calloway."

"We're not filming a documentary. I'm limiting this taping to five minutes. The clock starts as soon as the cameraman clears the door of the store. He will be so instructed."

"I think that will be agreeable. Ronnie and Sabra should be able to get their message across in that amount of time."

"I'm going to tell Kip to pan—"

"No, no," she interrupted quickly. "The baby's doing fine. I'll see to it that Kip gets close-ups of her."

"You're saying not to tape the interior of the store?"

"That's right. She's beautiful. Sleeping just now."

"I'm...uh..." Calloway wasn't sure what she was trying to communicate to him. After the Cain debacle, he couldn't afford any more mistakes.

"What's she saying?" Gully wanted to know.

"She doesn't want us to video the store's interior." Then: "Ms. McCoy, I'm going to put you on speaker." He depressed the button.

"Tiel, it's Gully. How're you doing, kid?"

"Gully! You're here?"

"Can you believe it? Me, who never gets more than ten miles from the TV station, out here in jackrabbit country. Mode of transportation was a helicopter. Noisiest goddamn contraption I've ever had the misfortune to fly in. Wouldn't let me smoke during the flight. This entire day has sucked. How're you?"

"I'm all right."

"Soon as you're out of there, the margaritas are on me."

"I'll take you up on that."

"Calloway's confused. You don't want Kip to pan the store's interior?"

"That's right."

"Freak everybody out?"

"Possibly."

"Okay. How about a wide shot?"

"That's very important, yes."

"Got it. Wide shot, but nobody's aware of it. Pretend they're close-ups. Is that what you're saying?"

"I can always count on you, Gully. We'll be watching for Kip." She hung up.

"You heard her," Gully said, heading for the door of the van to instruct the photographer waiting outside. "You'll get your interior shot, Mr. Calloway, but for whatever reason, Tiel doesn't want everyone to know they're on camera."

Chapter 11

Tiel consulted her compact mirror, but she snapped it shut without primping.

She reasoned that the more disheveled she looked, the more impact the video would have. Swapping her stained blouse for the T-shirt was the only concession she made. If viewers saw her as they usually did—well coiffed, well dressed, and cosmetically enhanced—the video would lose some of its punch.

She wanted it to pack a wallop. Not only with home viewers, but with the TV station's powers-that-be. This opportunity had been handed to her, and she intended to capitalize on it. While she already had a wonderful job and was highly respected for her journalistic instincts and know-how, her career would take a dramatic upward turn if she got the coveted hostess spot on *Nine Live*.

The daily news-magazine show had been in the planning stages for months. At first it was thought to be only a rumor, the pipe dream of station management, something on their wish list for the unspecified future.

But it now appeared that it was actually going to come about. The half-hour program was scheduled to air between *Jeopardy!* and the first edition of the evening news. Set designers were submitting drawings for review. Brainstorming sessions had been convened to discuss the show's concept, thrust, and focus. The promotions department was working on a distinctive, readily identifiable logo. A full-scale, saturating advertising campaign had been budgeted. *Nine Live* was soon to become a reality.

Tiel wanted it to be her reality, her future.

This story would be a boon to her chances of landing that job. This standoff would be a huge story tomorrow and probably for several days to come. Follow-up reports on the people involved could be produced indefinitely and the possibilities were endless: How Katherine was faring; Ronnie's trial and sentencing; the Davison-Dendy Standoff—a retrospective one year later.

She could do interviews with Special Agent Calloway, the Dendys, Ronnie's father, and Sheriff Montez. And the elusive Dr. Bradley Stanwick.

Of course it remained to be seen if Doc would agree to an interview, but anything was possible, and Tiel was an optimist.

For the next few days and weeks, she would be in the glare of the broadcast media spotlight. No doubt she would get a lot of ink, too, in newspapers and periodicals. The TV station would benefit hugely from her national exposure. Ratings would soar. She would be the darling of the newsroom, and her popularity would extend to the carpeted offices upstairs.

Eat your heart out, Linda Harper.

Ronnie interrupted her reverie. "Ms. McCoy? Is this him?"

The videographer materialized out of the shadows beyond the gasoline pumps. The camera weighted down his right arm, but it was also like an extension of it. He was rarely seen without it. "Yes, that's Kip."

Mentally she rehearsed what she was going to say as an open. *This is Tiel McCoy, speaking to you from inside a convenience store in Rojo Flats, Texas, where a drama involving two Fort Worth teenagers has been unfolding for the last several hours. As already reported, earlier today Ronnie Davison and Sabra Dendy...*

What was that? A twinge of conscience? She ignored it. This was her job. This is what she did. Just as Dr. Stanwick had applied his skill to the emergency birth, she was now applying her particular skill to the situation. What was wrong with that? It wasn't exploitation.

It wasn't!

If Sam Donaldson found himself on a hijacked airliner and had an opportunity to feed a story to his network, would he decline to do so just because the lives of other people were in jeopardy? Hell, no. Would he tell the head honcho at his network that he didn't want to do the story at the risk of invading the privacy of his fellow hostages? Don't make me laugh.

People made news. The most compelling stories were about people whose lives were in peril. The more immediate the danger, the more gripping the story. She hadn't created this situation to further her career. She was merely reporting on it. Sure, her career would benefit, but still, she was only doing her job.

Earlier today Ronnie Davison and Sabra Dendy fled their high school in defiance of parental authority—and ultimately in defiance of the law. These two young people are now engaged in a standoff with the FBI and other law enforcement agencies. I am one of their hostages.

Kip was at the door.

"How do I know he hasn't got a gun?" Ronnie asked nervously.

"He's a genius with a video camera, but I doubt he would know which end of a gun to point." It was true. Kip looked about as menacing as a marshmallow. Through a viewfinder, he saw the lighting and angles that would produce beautiful moving pictures. But he was woefully myopic when it came to seeing himself in a mirror. Or so it seemed. He was endearingly sloppy and ill-groomed.

Ronnie signaled Donna to activate the electronic lock. Kip pushed his way inside. The door was relocked behind him. He jumped nervously when he heard the metallic click.

"Hi, Kip."

"Tiel. You okay? Gully's wound up tighter than an eight-day clock."

"As you can see, I'm fine. Let's not waste time. This is Ronnie Davison."

Obviously Kip had expected a rough-looking thug, not the clean-cut, all-American boy Ronnie personified. "Hey."

"Hi."

"Where's the girl?" Kip asked.

"Lying down over there."

He looked in Sabra's direction and hitched his chin in greeting. "Hey."

Katherine was asleep in her mother's arms. Tiel noted that Doc was still sitting on the floor with his back to the freezer, where he could easily monitor Sabra but remain concealed by a revolving rack of snack food.

"Better get started," Kip said. "That Calloway was hyper about this taking no more than five minutes."

"I've got a few remarks to make first by way of intro, then you can tape Ronnie's statement. We'll save Sabra and the baby for last."

Kip handed Tiel the wireless microphone, then swung the camera up onto his shoulder and fitted the viewfinder against his eye socket. The light mounted on top of the camera came on. Tiel took up a preplanned position, where the majority of the store's interior could be seen behind her. "Is this okay?"

"Fine by me. Sound level's okay. I'm rolling."

"This is Tiel McCoy." She made the brief opening remarks she had rehearsed. Her statement of the facts was impassioned but not maudlin, having just the right blend of empathy and professional detachment. She resisted the temptation to embellish, believing that Ronnie and Sabra's comments would be more stirring than anything she could say.

When she finished, she signaled Ronnie forward. He seemed reluctant to move into the bright light. "How do I know they won't take a shot at me?"

"While you're on camera and posing no immediate threat? The FBI has enough of a PR problem without the public outcry that would create."

Apparently he saw the logic in Tiel's argument. Moving into place, he cleared his throat. "Tell me when to go."

"You're on," said Kip. "Go."

"I didn't kidnap Sabra Dendy," he blurted. "We ran away. Simple as that. It was wrong of me to rob this store. I admit that." He went on to explain that they had been driven away by Mr. Dendy's threat to separate them permanently from each other and their baby. "Sabra and I want to get married and live together with Katherine as a family. That's all. Mr. Dendy, if you won't let us live our own lives, we'll end them right here. Tonight."

"Two minutes," Kip whispered, reminding them of the time limit.

"Very good, Ronnie." Tiel took the microphone from him and signaled Kip to follow her to where Sabra lay. Quickly he positioned himself above her for the best possible camera angle.

"Be sure you're getting the baby, too," Sabra told him.

"Yes, ma'am. I'm rolling."

Ronnie had taken a typically masculine approach— aggressive, contentious, challenging. Sabra's statement was perhaps more eloquent, but equally and chillingly resolute. Tears welled up in her eyes, but she didn't falter when she concluded with, "It's impossible for you to un- derstand how we feel, Daddy, because you don't know what it's like to love someone. You say you only want what's best for me, but that's not true. You want what's best for you. You're willing to sacrifice me, you're willing to give up your granddaughter, just to have your way. That's sad. I don't hate you. I pity you."

She ended just as Kip said, "Time's up." He turned off the camera and lowered it from his shoulder. "I don't want to go over the time limit and be the cause of all hell breaking loose."

As he and Tiel picked their way back toward the door, he said, "A guy named Joe Marcus has called the newsroom several times."

"Who?"

"Joe Mar—"

"Oh, Joseph."

"He was making such a pest of himself they finally patched him through to me here."

"How'd he know about this?"

"Same as everybody else, I guess," Kip replied. "Heard it on the news. Wanted to know if you were all right. Said he was worried sick about you."

In the intervening hours since her telephone conversation with him, she'd almost forgotten the wife-cheating, lying rat with whom she had planned to spend a romantic holiday. It seemed a very long time ago that Joseph Marcus had held any appeal for her. She could barely remember what he looked like.

"If he calls again, hang up on him."

The unflappable photographer shrugged laconically. "Whatever."

"And Kip, be sure and tell Calloway and company that Agent Cain and the rest of us are faring well."

"Speak for yourself," Cain said. "You tell Calloway that I said—"

"Shut up!" Ronnie yelled at him. "Or I'll let that Mexican muzzle you again."

"Go to hell."

Kip looked reluctant to leave Tiel in such a hostile environment, but a pair of headlights flashed twice. "That's my signal," he explained. "Gotta go. Take care, Tiel."

He slipped through the door and Ronnie motioned Donna to lock it behind him.

Cain started laughing. "You're a fool, Davison. You think that video means doodle-dee-squat? Calloway only saw a way to stall a little longer, get more manpower in here."

Ronnie's eyes sawed between the FBI agent and Tiel, who shook her head. "I don't think so, Ronnie. You've talked to Calloway. He sounds sincerely concerned for everyone. I don't believe he would trick you."

"Then you're no smarter than he is." Cain snickered. "Calloway's got a psychologist out there, coaching him on how to deal with this situation. They know how to smooth-talk. They know which buttons to push. Calloway's got over twenty years in the Bureau. This standoff is chicken feed to him. He could handle it in his sleep."

"Why don't you shut up?" Ronnie said angrily.

"Why don't you eat shit?"

Vern, who'd come awake for the TV camera, said, "Hey, watch your language in front of my wife."

"Never mind, Vern," Gladys said. "He's an asshole."

"I gotta go to the john," Donna whined.

"I want everybody to settle down and be quiet!" Ronnie yelled.

He looked haggard. He had composed himself for the camera, but now his nerves were beginning to fray again. Fatigue, jangled nerves, and a loaded handgun made for a lethal combination.

Tiel could strangle Cain for goading him. In her opinion, the FBI would be better off without Agent Cain. "Ronnie, how about allowing us a bathroom break?" she suggested. "It's been hours for all of us. It may help everyone relax until we hear back from Calloway. What do you say?"

He thought it over. "You ladies. One at a time. Not the men. If they have to go, they can do it out here."

Donna excused herself first. Then Gladys. Tiel went last. While in the rest room, she rewound the audiotape in her pocket recorder and spot-checked it. Sabra's voice came through, muffled but distinct enough, saying about her father, "That's the kind of person he is. He hates to be crossed." She fast-forwarded, stopped it again, depressed the Play button, and heard Doc's gritty baritone. "...at everybody. At everything. Goddamn cancer. My own inadequacy."

Yes! She'd been afraid the tape had run out before that confidential conversation. He would be a fantastic guest to have on *Nine Live*. If she could persuade him to do it. She would just have to, that's all. She would begin the program with file footage of his travails following his wife's death, then ask for an updated viewpoint on those unhappy events that had reshaped his life. They could segue into a discussion about destroyed dreams. A psychologist, possibly a clergyman, could join them to expand on that theme: What happens to one's spirit when one's world falls apart?

Excited by the prospect, she replaced the recorder in her pocket, used the toilet, and washed her face and hands. By the time she came out, Vern was headed toward the men's room to empty the bucket the men had used. As Vern passed Cain, he asked Ronnie, "What about him?"

"No. Unless you're volunteering to unzip him and do the honors."

Vern snorted and continued on his way. "Looks like you're gonna have to wet yourself, G-man."

The Mexican men, catching the gist of the exchange, snorted with ridicule.

Tiel rejoined Doc, whose gaze was fixed on the two men seated near the refrigerated cabinet with the shattered glass door. Tiel followed the direction of his thoughtful stare. "I wonder about that," he murmured.

"What?"

"The two of them."

"Juan and Two?"

"Pardon?"

"I nicknamed the short one Juan. The taller one—"

"Two. I get it."

He turned away and resumed his spot near Sabra. Tiel looked at him quizzically as she sat down beside him. "What's bothering you about them?"

He raised one shoulder in a shrug. "Something's out of joint."

"Like what?"

"I can't put my finger on it. I noticed them when they first came into the store. They were acting weird even then."

"In what way?"

"They were heating up food in the microwave, but I got the impression they weren't really here for a snack. It was like they were killing time. Waiting on something. Or someone."

"Hmm."

"I picked up this...I don't know...bad vibe." He chuckled with self-deprecation. "I was leery of them, but never in a million years would I have looked twice at Ronnie Davison. Just goes to show how misleading first impressions can be."

"Oh, I'm not so sure about that. I noticed you when you came into the store."

Inquisitively, he arched an eyebrow.

The directness of his stare was both exciting and unsettling. It caused a fluttering in her tummy. "You cast an imposing silhouette, Doc, especially with your hat on."

"Oh. Yeah. I've always been tall for my age."

It was meant as a joke, and it worked to the extent that Tiel was able to resume breathing.

Then he said, "Thanks for honoring my request not to be on camera."

Conscience was more than a twinge this time. It was

a jabbing needle and much harder to ignore. She mumbled an appropriate response, then, eager to change the subject, gestured toward Sabra. "Any change?"

"Bleeding's increased again. Not as bad as before. I should get her to nurse the baby again. It's been over an hour, but I hate to disturb her while she's sleeping."

"They're probably already watching that video. Maybe she'll be in a hospital soon."

"She's a trooper. But she's exhausted."

"So is Ronnie. I see signs of disintegration. I wish I hadn't watched all those dramas about hostage situations—fiction and non. The longer something like this drags on, the more excitable everyone becomes. Nerves snap. Tempers flare."

"Then guns."

"Don't even say it." She shuddered. "For an instant there, I was afraid that Ronnie's concern about sharpshooters was valid. What if Calloway had buffaloed me? Agreeing to do the video could have been a setup in which Kip, Gully, and I were pawns."

Adjusting himself into a more comfortable position, he asked, "Who's this Gully?"

She described their working relationship. "He's a real character. I'll bet he's giving them fits out there," she said with a smile.

"And who's Joe?"

The unexpected question pulled the plug on her smile. "Nobody."

"Somebody. Boyfriend?"

"A wanna-be."

"A wanna-be boyfriend?"

Piqued by his persistence, she was about to tell him to mind his own business and to stop eavesdropping on her private conversations. But in view of the audiocassette in her possession, she rethought her reaction. A good way to win his confidence would be to confide in him.

"Joseph and I had several dates. Joseph was on his way to earning the official designation of 'boyfriend,' but Joseph failed to mention that he was another woman's husband. I made that rude discovery this very afternoon."

"Hmm. Mad?"

"You betcha. Furious."

"Regrets?"

"Over him? No. None at all. Over being such a gullible goose, yes." She hammered her fist into her palm as though it were a judge's gavel. "From now on, all future dates are required to tender no less than three notarized character references."

"What about your ex?"

Score two for Doc. He had a real knack for instantly deflating her smiles with an abrupt and sobering question. "What about him?"

"Is he a consideration?"

"No."

"Are you sure?"

"Of course I'm sure."

"No lingering—"

"No."

He frowned doubtfully. "You looked awfully funny when I mentioned him."

Inwardly she was pleading with him not to put her through this. By the same token, telling the story would serve him right for being so nosy.

"John Malone. Great TV name, huh? With a face and a voice to go with it. We met through work and fell hopelessly in love. The first few months were bliss. Then shortly after we were married, he was hired by one of the networks to be a foreign correspondent."

"Ah. I see."

"No, you don't," she retorted. "Not at all. Professional jealousy didn't factor in. It was a fantastic opportunity for John, and I was foursquare in favor of it. The thought of living abroad was enticing. I envisioned Paris or London or Rome. But his choice came down to either South America or Bosnia. This was before most Americans had even heard of Bosnia. The struggle there was just beginning."

Absently she picked at a loose thread on the hem of the T-shirt. "Naturally, I urged him to take the safer choice—Rio. Where, incidentally, I could go with him. I didn't relish the thought of my groom leaving me Stateside and going into a war zone, particularly one where boundaries were imprecise and everyone was still choosing up sides.

"He opted for the more thrilling of the two. He wanted to be where the action was, where he would be guaranteed more airtime. We argued about it. Virulently. Finally I said, 'All right, John, fine. Go. Get yourself killed.' "

Raising her head, she met Doc's eyes directly. "And that's what he did."

His expression remained impassive.

Tiel plunged on. "He had gone into an area where journalists weren't supposed to go—which didn't surprise me," she added on a soft laugh. "He was an adventurer by nature. Anyway, he caught a sniper bullet. They shipped his body home. I buried him three months shy of our first wedding anniversary."

After a time, Doc said, "That's tough. I'm sorry."

"Yes, well…"

They were silent for a long while. It was Tiel who finally spoke. "What's it been like for you?"

"In regards to what?"

"Relationships."

"Specifically...?"

"Come on, Doc. Don't play dumb," she chided softly. "I was candid with you."

"Which was your choice."

"Fair's fair. Share with me."

"There's nothing to share."

"About you and women?" she asked incredulously. "I don't believe that."

"What do you want? Names and dates? Starting when, Ms. McCoy? Does high school count, or should I begin with college?"

"How about since your wife died?"

"How about you mind your own fucking business?"

"Actually we're talking about your fucking business."

"No, *we're* not. *You* are."

"In light of your wife's affair, I think you'd find it difficult to trust another woman."

His mouth compressed into a tight, angry line, indicating that she'd struck a tender nerve. "You don't know anything about—"

But Tiel never learned from him what she didn't know anything about because he was interrupted by Donna's ear-splitting scream.

Chapter 12

K ip's videotape was playing simultaneously on two monitors in the van, with everyone inside clustered around to view them. One of the FBI agents was manning the control panel, standing by to freeze the picture at Calloway's command.

"Where's my daughter? I don't see Sabra."

Calloway detected liquor on Dendy's breath. Periodically he had been stepping outside "to get some fresh air." It seemed he was taking in more than oxygen.

"Patience, Mr. Dendy. We're anxious to see all of it. I need to know where people are positioned. Once I have an overview, we'll restart the tape and pause it on the segments that warrant closer study."

"Maybe Sabra tried to send me a private message. Like a signal."

"Maybe," was the senior agent's noncommittal reply.

His nose was no farther than ten inches from the color monitor as he listened to Tiel McCoy's opening remarks. She was poised, he'd give her that. Unruffled.

She looked a little worse for wear in her Texas flag T-shirt, but she was as composed and articulate as she would have been in a television studio, safely behind a sleek news desk.

"That son of a bitch," Dendy snarled when Ronnie appeared on the screen.

"If you can't keep your mouth shut, Dendy, I'll be happy to shut it for you." Cole Davison issued the threat in a soft voice, but there was muscle behind it.

"Gentlemen," Calloway said.

No one else spoke while Ronnie was delivering his speech. But the silence became even heavier when the camera moved to Sabra and her newborn. The images were poignant, heart-rending. The dialogue was disturbing. No new mother cradling her infant should be threatening to take her own life.

For several seconds after the tape ended, no one spoke. Finally Gully had the courage to say out loud what everyone else was thinking. "Guess that settles the question as to who's responsible for all this."

Calloway held up his hand, discouraging any further unsolicited editorial comments on Russell Dendy's culpability. He turned to Cole Davison. "What about Ronnie? How does he seem to you?"

"Exhausted. Scared."

"High?"

"No, sir," Davison replied briskly. "I told you, he's a good boy. He doesn't do drugs. Maybe a beer now and then. That's the extent of it."

"My daughter certainly isn't a druggie," Dendy remarked.

Calloway remained centered on Davison. "Did you see anything unusual that should alert us to an unstable state of mind?"

"My eighteen-year-old son is talking about killing himself, Mr. Calloway. I think that sums up his state of mind."

While Calloway sympathized with the man—he had teenagers of his own—he pressured him for more information. "You know him, Mr. Davison. Do you think Ronnie is bluffing? Does he sound sincere to you? Do you believe he would go through with it?"

The man wrestled with his answer. Then he lowered his head dejectedly. "No, I don't think so. Truly, I don't. But—"

"But?" Calloway pounced on the qualifier. "But what? Has Ronnie ever shown suicidal tendencies?"

"Never."

"A violent streak? Uncontrollable temper?"

"No," he replied shortly. However, he appeared uncomfortable with his preemptive answer. Nervously his eyes shifted from Calloway to the others, then back to the agent. "Well, only one time. It was an isolated incident. And he was just a kid."

Inwardly Calloway groaned. He was very sure he didn't want to hear about the one time Ronnie Davison had lost it. "It may not be relevant—probably isn't—but maybe you'd better tell me about it."

After a long, uneasy silence, Davison began. "Ronnie was staying with me during his summer vacation. It hadn't been long since his mother and I had divorced. Ronnie was having trouble adjusting to the split. Anyway," he said, shifting his feet self-consciously, "he took a shine to this dog that lived a few blocks over. He told me her owner was mean to her, didn't always feed her, never bathed her. Stuff like that.

"I knew the owner. He was a mean ol' bastard, drunk most of the time, so I knew Ronnie was telling the truth.

But it was none of our business. I told Ronnie to stay away from the dog. But, as I said, he'd formed a real attachment to the mangy thing. I guess he needed a companion. Or maybe he liked the animal because it was as miserable as he was that summer. I don't know. I'm no child psychologist."

Dendy interrupted. "Is this sad story going anywhere?"

Calloway shot him a look and came close to telling him to shut up before turning back to the other man. "What happened, Cole?"

"One day Ronnie unchained the dog and brought her to our house. I told him to return her to the neighbor's backyard immediately. He started crying and refused to. Said he'd rather see her dead than living like that. I scolded him and went to get my keys, meaning to drive the dog home in my pickup.

"But when I came back through the kitchen, Ronnie was gone and so was the dog. Long story short, I searched for them all night. Had neighbors and friends out looking for him, too. Early the next morning a rancher spotted him and the dog hiding behind his barn and called the sheriff.

"As we converged on the barn, I called out to Ronnie, telling him that it was time to take the dog back to her owner and go home. He shouted back that he wasn't going to give the dog up, that he wouldn't let her be mistreated the way she'd been."

He stopped speaking and stared at the brim of his hat as he slowly threaded it through his fingers. "When we came around to the back to the barn, he was crying his heart out. He was patting the dog where it was lying right there beside him. Dead. He'd hit it in the head with a rock and killed it."

The eyes he raised to Calloway were red with threatened tears. "Mr. Calloway, I asked my boy how he could have done such a horrible thing. He told me he'd done it because he loved the dog so much." His wide chest shuddered when he deeply inhaled. "Sorry I got so long-winded. But you asked if I thought he could possibly do what he says he'll do. That's the best way I know to answer you."

Calloway curbed the unprofessional impulse to press the man's shoulder. Instead he said tersely, "Thank you for the insight."

"So he's a head case," Dendy muttered. "Just like I said all along."

Although Dendy's remark was unnecessarily cruel, Calloway couldn't entirely disagree with the connotation. This incident from Ronnie's childhood dangerously paralleled the present circumstances. Cole Davison's story added another factor to the situation, and it wasn't a positive one. In fact, none of the factors had been positive since this standoff began. Not one.

He turned to Gully. "What about Ms. McCoy? Did you see any signs that suggest she's under duress? Is she trying to get across more than she's saying? Any double meanings to her words?"

"Not that I could tell. And I grilled Kip here real good."

The FBI agent turned to the video cameraman. "Everything was as they've told us? Nobody hurt?"

"No, sir. The FBI guy is tied up—taped, rather—but he's shooting off his mouth, so I guess he's all right." He glanced at Dendy apprehensively, as though remembering what happens to the bearers of bad news. "But the . . . the girl?"

"Sabra? What about her?"

"There were a lot of bloody disposable diapers

around. They were wadded up and pushed aside. But I remember seeing them and thinking, *Jeez*."

Dendy strangled on an anguished exclamation.

Calloway continued with Kip. "Did you notice anything in your co-worker's manner or delivery that was out of the ordinary?"

"Tiel was same as always. Well, except for looking like hell. She was cool as a cucumber, though."

Finally the senior agent turned to Dendy, who had skipped the trip outside and was openly drinking from a silver pocket flask. "You mentioned the possibility of Sabra sending you a secret message. Did you see or hear anything to suggest one?"

"How could I tell by seeing the tape only that one time?"

The fact that the tyrannical entrepreneur was uneasy and indirect with his answer was in itself telling. Dendy finally had been confronted with the ugly truth: His mishandling of the original predicament had prompted Sabra and Ronnie to take desperate measures, which had gone terribly awry.

"Rewind it," Calloway instructed the agent at the control panel. "Let's watch the tape again. Anybody notice anything, call out." The tape began again.

"Tiel picked that spot so we could see the people behind her," Gully remarked.

"That's the refrigerator where the door was shattered," one of the other agents said, pointing to a spot on the screen.

"Pause it there."

Leaning forward, Calloway focused not on the newswoman but on the group of people in the background. "The woman leaning against the counter must be the cashier."

Sheriff Montez said, "That's Donna, all right. No mistaking that hairdo."

"And that's Agent Cain, right, Kip?" Calloway pointed to a pair of legs, which he could see only from the knees down.

"Right. He's sitting with his back to the counter."

"Silver duct tape sure shows up good against his black pants, doesn't it?"

Gully's sly gibe went unacknowledged. Calloway was studying the elderly couple sitting close together on the floor near Cain. "How about the old folks? Are they all right?"

"Wide-eyed and bushy-tailed from what I could tell."

"What about the other two men?"

"Mexican fellows. I heard one of them say something to the other in Spanish, but he was talking under his breath, and I wouldn't've understood it anyhow."

"Oh, Jesus." Calloway sprang far forward in his chair so quickly the casters sent it rolling from beneath him.

"What?"

The other agents, responding to their superior's apparent alarm, pushed the others aside and crowded around him. "This one." Calloway tapped the monitor screen. "Take a good look and tell me if he looks familiar. Can you bring him in any closer?"

Using the technology available, the agent manning the controls isolated the Mexican man's face. He was able to enlarge the image, but doing so sacrificed quality and focus. The agents squinted at the grainy picture, then one of them snapped his head around and exclaimed, "Ah, *shit!*"

"What?" Dendy demanded.

Davison jumped in. "What's the matter?" Calloway shoved them aside and began issuing orders to his subordinates. "Call the office. Get everyone mobilized. Put out an APB—Montez, your men can help."

"Sure. But help what?" The sheriff raised his arms at his sides in a helpless shrug. "Y'all have lost me."

"Round up all your deputies. Notify neighboring counties as well. Tell them to start looking for an abandoned truck. Railroad car. Moving van."

"Truck? Moving van? What the hell is going on?" Dendy had to shout to make himself heard above the confusion that Calloway's galvanizing orders had created in the cramped van. "What about my daughter?"

"Sabra, all of them, are in more danger than we thought."

As though to underscore Calloway's distressing words, they heard the unmistakable crack of gunfire.

———◦◦◦———

Donna's blood-curdling scream brought Tiel to her feet. "What now?"

Ronnie was brandishing his pistol and shouting, "Get back! Get back! I'll shoot you!"

Two, the taller of the Mexicans, had charged him. Ronnie had halted him at gunpoint. "Where's the other one?" he shouted frantically. "Where's your buddy?"

Sabra screamed. "No! No!"

Tiel whirled around in time to see Juan snatch Katherine from Sabra's arms. He clutched the newborn tightly—too tightly—against his chest. The infant began squalling, but Sabra was shrieking as only a mother whose child is in danger can shriek. She was struggling to stand, clawing at Juan's pants legs, as though to climb them.

"Sabra!" Ronnie cried. "What's wrong?"

"He has the baby! Give me my baby! Don't hurt her!"

Tiel lunged forward, but Juan thrust out his hand and the heel of it caught her in the sternum, forcing her back. She cried out in pain and fear for the newborn.

Doc shouted a wordless protest, but Tiel reasoned that he was afraid to charge Juan because of what he might do to the infant in retaliation.

"Tell him to give her the baby!" Ronnie was clutching the pistol in both hands, aiming it directly at Two's chest and yelling at the top of his lungs, as though volume could conquer the language barrier. "Tell your friend to give her the baby, or I'll kill you!"

Perhaps to see just how earnest Ronnie's threat was, Juan made the mistake of glancing toward the front of the store where the two were facing off.

Doc used that split second to make a lunge for him.

But the Mexican reacted instantly. He executed a practiced uppercut that made a significant dent in Doc's belly. Doc bent in half at the waist, then collapsed to the floor in front of the freezer.

"Tell him to give her the baby!" Ronnie repeated in a shrill voice that splintered like thin ice.

Donna wailed, "We're all gonna die."

Tiel was begging Juan not to harm Katherine. "Don't hurt her. She's no threat to you. Give the baby to her mother. Please. Please, don't do this."

Sabra was practically helpless. Nevertheless, maternal instinct propelled her to her feet. She was so weak she could barely stand. Swaying slightly, hand outstretched, she implored the man to return her baby to her.

Juan and Two were shouting back and forth to one another, trying to communicate above the other voices, including those of Vern and Gladys, who was cursing a blue streak. Donna was caterwauling. Agent Cain was shouting accusations at Ronnie, saying that if he had surrendered earlier this wouldn't have happened, that if the standoff resulted in tragedy it was no one's fault but his own.

The gunshot rendered everyone speechless.

Tiel, who had been appealing to Juan, witnessed his grimace when the bullet struck. Reflexively, he pitched forward and grabbed his thigh. He would have dropped Katherine if Tiel hadn't been there to catch her.

Holding the baby close, she spun around, wondering how Ronnie had managed to get off such a clear and accurate shot, one so well placed that it had disabled Juan but hadn't endangered the baby.

But Ronnie still had the bore of his pistol trained on Two's chest and seemed as surprised as anyone that a gun had been fired.

Doc had been the marksman. He was lying on his back on the floor, a small revolver in his hand. Tiel recognized Agent Cain's weapon, the one she had kicked beneath the freezer and forgotten. Thank God Doc had remembered it.

He took advantage of the momentary silence. "Gladys, get over here."

The old lady came scurrying around the Frito-Lay display. "Did you kill him?"

"No."

"Too bad."

"Take the baby so Tiel can tend to Sabra. I'll take care of him," he said, referring to Juan. "Ronnie, relax. Everything's under control. No need to panic."

"Is the baby okay?"

"She's fine." Gladys carried the crying infant over to

where Ronnie could see her for himself. "She's mad as hell, and I can't say as I blame her." Glaring back at Juan where he now sat on the floor gripping his bleeding thigh, she snarled with contempt.

Several jabs of Ronnie's pistol sent Two skulking back to his original spot. His expression was meaner and more agitated than before.

Doc placed Cain's revolver high on a grocery shelf, well out of Juan's reach, and knelt down to cut open his trouser leg with the scissors. "You'll live," he said laconically after assessing the damage and stuffing gauze pads into the wound. "Lucky for you the bullet missed the femoral artery."

Juan's eyes blazed with resentment.

"Doc?" Tiel had got Sabra to lie back down, but fresh blood was making the floor around her slick. The girl was ghastly pale.

"I know," Doc said soberly, picking up on Tiel's unspoken alarm. "I'm sure she reopened the tear in the perineum. Make her as comfortable as you can. I'll be right back."

He had hurriedly bandaged Juan's wound and fashioned a tourniquet with another of the souvenir T-shirts. Evidently in excruciating pain, Juan was sweating profusely, and his straight, white teeth were clenched. But, to his credit, he didn't cry out when Doc unceremoniously and none too gently hoisted him to his feet and supported him as he hopped on one foot.

As they went past Cain, the agent addressed the gunshot man. "You goddamn fool. You could've got us all killed. What were you—"

Quicker than a striking rattlesnake, Juan, using the foot of his injured leg, kicked Cain viciously in the head. The sudden move cost him dearly. He grunted with pain. Even so, his boot heel had connected solidly with bone, and the snapping sound was almost as loud as the pistol shot. Cain went silent and unconscious in the same instant. His chin dropped forward onto his chest.

Doc pushed Juan to the floor, propping him against the refrigerator well away from his confederate. "He's not going anywhere. But just to be safe, better bind his hands, Ronnie. His too," he added, motioning toward Two.

Ronnie instructed Vern to tape the two men's hands and feet like Cain's. He held the pistol on them while the old man went about the task. Juan was too involved with his injured leg to waste energy on invectives, but Two was under no such constraints. He kept up a litany of what was presumed to be Spanish vulgarities until Ronnie threatened to gag him if he didn't shut up.

The ringing telephone had gone unanswered and largely ignored. Tiel, who had snapped on a pair of gloves with an alacrity that amazed her, was working frantically to replace the blood-soaked diaper beneath Sabra, when the phone suddenly stopped ringing and she heard Ronnie shout, "Not now, we're busy!" before slamming the receiver back into the cradle. Then he called, "How's Sabra?"

Tiel addressed him over her shoulder. "Not good." She was vastly relieved to see Doc returning. "What's going on?"

"Juan kicked Cain in the head. He's unconscious."

"I never thought I'd be thanking that man for anything."

"Vern is binding them. I'm glad they're...contained."

She noticed the intensity in his face, and knew that Sabra's worsening condition wasn't the only reason for it.

"Because they're loose cannons? They really had nothing to lose by trying to seize control of the situation."

"True. But what did they have to gain?"

Did Ronnie Davison really represent a threat to tough-looking *hombres* like them? After thinking about it, she said, "Nothing that I can see."

"Nothing that you can *see*. That's what bothers me. There's more," he continued in a lower voice. "Men with rifles have taken up position outside. Probably a SWAT team."

"Oh, no."

"I saw them moving into place and taking cover."

"Has Ronnie seen them?"

"I don't think so. That shot I fired must've got everyone nervous. They're probably thinking the worst. They might storm the building, try coming in through the roof or something."

"He would freak."

"That's my point."

The telephone rang again. "Ronnie, answer it," Doc called to him. "Explain to them what happened."

"Not until I know Sabra's all right."

Although Tiel wasn't a medical expert by any means, Sabra's condition appeared critical to her. But, like Doc, she didn't want Ronnie any more frazzled than he already was.

"Where's Katherine?" the girl asked weakly.

Doc, who had done his best to stem the flow of fresh blood, peeled off his glove and smoothed her hair away from her forehead. "Gladys is taking good care of her. She's rocked her to sleep. Seems to me that baby girl is as brave as her mother."

Even a smile seemed too much of an effort for her. "We're not going to get out of here, are we?"

"Don't say that, Sabra," Tiel whispered fiercely, watching Doc's face as he read the blood-pressure gauge. "Don't even think it."

"Daddy's not going to give up. Neither am I. And neither is Ronnie. He can't now anyway. If he did, they'd just put him in jail."

She divided a glassy, hollow-eyed gaze between Tiel and Doc. "Tell Ronnie to come over here. I want to talk to him. Now. I don't want to wait any longer."

Although she didn't specifically mention their suicide pact, her meaning was clear. Tiel's chest grew tight with anxiety and despair. "We can't let you do it, Sabra. You know it's wrong. It's not the answer."

"Please help us. It's what we want."

Then, of their own volition and against her will, her eyes closed. She was too weak to reopen them and lapsed into a doze.

Tiel looked across at Doc. "It's bad, isn't it?"

"Very. Blood pressure's dropping. Pulse is high. She's going to bleed out."

"What are we going to do?"

Sternly staring into the girl's pale, still face, he thought on it a moment, then said, "I'll tell you what I'm going to do."

He stood up, retrieved the pistol from the shelf, stepped around the Frito-Lay display, and approached Ronnie, who was waiting for an update on Sabra's condition.

Chapter 13

"Why aren't they answering the phone?" Events had reduced Dendy's characteristic bellow to a high-pitched squeal. He was beside himself.

Indeed, the gunshots had plunged everyone inside the van into a state of near panic. Cole Davison had rushed outside, only to return moments later, yelling at Calloway because the SWAT team had been mobilized.

"You promised! You said Ronnie wouldn't get hurt. If you pressure him, if he feels like you're closing in on him, he might...might do something like he did before."

"Calm down, Mr. Davison. I'm taking precautionary measures as I see fit." Calloway held the telephone receiver to his ear, but thus far his call into the convenience store had gone unanswered. "Can anybody see anything?"

"Movement," one of the other agents hollered. Via a headset, he was communicating with another agent outside who was equipped with binoculars. "Can't make out who's doing what."

"Keep me posted."

"Yes, sir. Are you going to tell the kid about Huerta?"

"Who's that?" Dendy wanted to know.

"Luis Huerta. One of our Ten Most Wanted." To the other agent, Calloway replied, "No, I'm not going to tell them. That might panic everyone, including Huerta. He's capable of just about anything."

Ronnie answered the phone. "Not now, we're busy!"

Calloway swore lavishly when the dial tone replaced Ronnie's frantic voice. He immediately redialed.

"One of the Mexicans in there is on the FBI's Ten Most Wanted list?" Cole Davison was becoming increasingly distraught. "What for? What'd he do?"

"He smuggles Mexican nationals across the border with promises of work visas and well-paying jobs, then sells them into slave labor. Last summer Border Patrol got tipped of a transport and were hot on his tail. Huerta and two of his henchmen, realizing they were about to be apprehended, abandoned the truck in the New Mexico desert and scattered like the cockroaches they are. All evaded capture.

"The van wasn't found for three days. Forty-five people—men, women, and children—had been locked in from the outside. The heat inside the trailer must've reached two hundred degrees or higher. Huerta is wanted on forty-five counts of murder and miscellaneous other felonies.

"For almost a year he's been holed up somewhere in Mexico. The authorities down there are cooperative and want him as badly as we do, but he's a cagey bastard. Only one thing could get him to risk exposure. Money. Lots of it. So if he's resurfaced here, then I'm guessing that somewhere in the general vicinity there's a shipment of people waiting to be sold."

Davison looked ready to heave his last meal. "Who's the man with him?"

"One of his bodyguards, I'm sure. They're dangerous, ruthless men, and their stock in trade is human beings. What puzzles me is why they aren't armed. Or if they are, why they haven't shot their way out before now."

Dendy's chest rose and fell, emitting a gurgling sound like a sob. "Listen, Calloway. I've been thinking."

Even though Calloway kept the telephone receiver to his ear, he gave Russell Dendy his full attention. He suspected that Dendy was tight. He'd been sipping at the flask throughout the evening. He appeared extremely upset, on the brink of losing control of his emotions. He was no longer being a belligerent pain in the ass.

"I'm listening, Mr. Dendy."

"Just get them out of there safely. That's what's important now. Tell Sabra she can keep the baby. I won't interfere. That videotape of my daughter..." He rubbed the back of his hand across leaking eyes. "It got to me. Nothing else matters anymore. I just want to see my daughter safely out of there."

"That's my goal too, Mr. Dendy," Calloway assured him.

"Agree to any of the boy's terms."

"I'll negotiate for him the best deal I can. But first, I've got to get him to talk to me."

The telephone continued to ring.

* * *

"Ronnie?"

The young man didn't realize that Doc was in possession of the pistol. Evidently, in all the confusion, Ronnie had forgotten about Cain's secreted weapon. Doc raised his hand, and, seeing the gun, the younger man flinched. Donna let out a squeak of fright before clapping both hands over her mouth.

But Doc palmed the short barrel and extended the grip toward Ronnie. "That's how much faith I have in you to make the right decision."

Looking terribly young, uncertain, and vulnerable, Ronnie took the gun and stuffed it into the waistband of his jeans. "You already know my decision, Doc."

"Suicide? That's not a decision. That's a chickenshit cop-out."

The boy blinked in surprise over the blunt language, but it served to shake his resolve, which Tiel surmised was Doc's intention. "I don't want to talk about it. Sabra and I have made up our minds."

"Answer the phone," Doc encouraged in a calm, persuasive voice. "Tell them what happened in here. They heard the shots. They don't know what the hell is going on, but they're probably thinking the worst. Allay their fears, Ronnie. Otherwise, at any second a SWAT team may come barging in here, and somebody will wind up bloody, possibly dead."

"What SWAT team? You're lying."

"Would I lie to you after handing you a loaded gun? Hardly. I saw men taking up positions while you were distracted by tying up those Mexican guys. The SWAT team is out there, itching for a signal from Calloway. Don't give him reason to activate them."

Ronnie glanced nervously through the plate glass, but he could see nothing except the growing number of official vehicles that had converged on the area and created a traffic jam on the highway.

"Let me answer the phone, Ronnie," Tiel suggested,

stepping forward to take advantage of his indecision. "Let's hear what they have to say about the video. Their reaction to it might have been very positive. They could be calling to agree to all your conditions."

"Okay," he muttered, motioning her toward the telephone.

She counted it a blessing to stop the infernal ringing. "It's Tiel," she said upon lifting the receiver.

"Ms. McCoy, who fired those shots? What's going on in there?"

Calloway's brusqueness conveyed his concern. Not wanting to keep him in suspense, as succinctly as possible she explained how Cain's pistol had come to be fired. "It was hairy there for a minute or two, but the situation is now under control again. The two men who caused the fracas have been contained," she said, using Doc's euphemistic terminology.

"You're referring to the two Mexican men?"

"That's correct."

"They're secure?"

"Correct again."

"And where is Agent Cain's pistol now?"

"Doc gave it to Ronnie."

"I beg your pardon?"

"As a sign of trust, Mr. Calloway," she said testily, in Doc's defense.

The FBI agent expelled a long breath. "That's a hell of a lot of trust, Ms. McCoy."

"It was the right thing to do. You'd have to be here to understand."

"Apparently," he said dryly.

While talking to Calloway, she'd been listening with one ear to Doc as he continued trying to persuade Ronnie to surrender. She heard him say, "You're a father now. You're responsible for your family. Sabra's condition is critical, and there's nothing more I can do for her."

Calloway asked, "You don't feel in danger of him?"

"Not at all."

"Are any of the hostages in danger?"

"Presently, no. I can't predict what will happen if those guys in body armor charge the place."

"I don't intend to give that order."

"Then why are they there?" He paused for a long moment, and Tiel got the uneasy and distinct impression that he was withholding something, something important. "Mr. Calloway, if there's something I should know—"

"We've had a change of heart."

"You're giving up and going away?" At this point, that would be her fondest wish.

Calloway ignored her facetiousness. "The videotape was effective. You'll be glad to learn that it achieved exactly what you hoped. Mr. Dendy was touched by his daughter's appeal and is now ready to make concessions. He wants this to end peaceably and safely. As we all do. What is Ronnie's current state of mind?"

"Doc's working on him."

"How is he responding?"

"Favorably, I think."

"Good. That's good."

He sounded relieved, and, again, Tiel got the impression that the federal agent was withholding something she'd be better off knowing.

"Do you think he'll go for total surrender?"

"He specified the conditions under which he would surrender, Mr. Calloway."

"Dendy will concede that this was a runaway and

not a kidnaping. Of course the additional charges would stand."

"And they must be allowed to keep their child."

"Dendy said as much himself a few minutes ago. If Davison will agree to those terms, he'll have my personal guarantee that no force will be used."

"I'll pass along the message and get back to you."

"I'm standing by."

She hung up. Ronnie and Doc turned to her. In fact, everyone was listening intently. It seemed that the role of mediator had been bestowed on her. She didn't particularly welcome it. Suppose, despite everyone's best intentions, something went terribly wrong? If this standoff ultimately ended in disaster, for the rest of her life she would feel responsible for the tragic outcome.

Over the course of the last few hours, Tiel's priority had shifted. It had been a gradual shift, and until this moment she hadn't even realized that it had taken place. The news story had become a secondary consideration. At what point had it become an afterthought? When she saw Sabra's blood on her gloved hands? When Juan threatened Katherine's fragile life?

The people making the story were much more important to her now than the story itself. Producing a prize-winning, job-securing exclusive account of this drama wasn't as vital a goal as it had been previously. What she wished for now was a resolution to celebrate, not lament. If she blew it...

She simply couldn't, that's all.

"The kidnaping allegation has been dropped," she told Ronnie, who was listening expectantly. "You'll have to face other criminal charges. Mr. Dendy has agreed to let Sabra keep the baby. If you agree to these terms and surrender, Mr. Calloway gives you his personal guarantee that no force will be used."

"It's a good deal, Ronnie," Doc said. "Take it."

"I—"

"No, don't."

Sabra spoke in hardly more than a croak. Somehow she had managed to stand. She was leaning heavily against the freezer chest in order to keep herself upright. Her eyes were sunken and her complexion was leeched of all color. She looked like someone who'd had theatrical makeup expertly applied for a character rising out of a coffin.

"It's a trick, Ronnie. One of Daddy's tricks."

Doc rushed over to lend her support. "I don't think so, Sabra. Your dad responded to the video message you sent him."

Gratefully she clung to Doc, but her dull eyes beseeched Ronnie. "If you love me, don't agree to this. I won't leave here until I know I can be with you forever."

"Sabra, what about your baby?" Tiel asked gently. "Think of her."

"You take her."

"What?"

"Carry her out. Give her to someone who'll take care of her. No matter what happens to us—to Ronnie and me—it's important to me to know that Katherine is going to be all right."

Tiel looked hopefully toward Doc for inspiration, but his expression was bleak. He seemed to feel as helpless as she.

"That's it then," Ronnie stated firmly. "That's what we'll do. We'll let you carry Katherine out. But we're not leaving until they let us go. Free and clear. No compromise."

"They'll never agree to that," Tiel said with desperation. "That's an unreasonable demand."

"You committed armed robbery," Doc added. "You'll have to account for that, Ronnie. But because of extenuating circumstances, you'd have a good chance of beating the rap. Running away would be the worst thing you could do. That would solve nothing."

Tiel glanced at Doc, wondering if he were listening to his own advice. The admonishment against running away could be applied to him and his circumstances three years ago. He didn't notice her glance, however, because his attention was on Ronnie, who was arguing his point.

"Sabra and I vowed that we would never be forced apart. No matter what, we promised each other to stay together. We meant it."

"Your father—"

"I'm not going to talk about it," the young man snapped. Turning to Tiel, he asked if she would carry Katherine out and deliver that message.

"What about the others? Will you release them?"

He glanced beyond her at the other hostages. "Not the two Mexicans. And not him," he said of Agent Cain. He had regained consciousness but appeared still to be incoherent from the kick in the head Juan had given him. "The old folks and her. They can go."

When he pointed to Donna, she clasped her claw-like hands beneath her chin. "Thank you, Lord."

"I don't want to go," Gladys announced. She was still holding the sleeping infant in her arms. "I want to see what's going to happen."

"We'd better do as he says," Vern said, patting her shoulder. "We can wait for everybody else outside." He assisted Gladys up off the floor. "Before we go, I'm sure Sabra wants to tell Katherine good-bye."

The old lady carried the baby over to Sabra, where she was leaning heavily against Doc.

"Shall I notify Calloway of your decision?" Tiel asked Ronnie.

He was watching Sabra and his baby. "Half an hour."

"What?"

"That's the time limit I'm giving them to get back to me. If they won't let us leave in half an hour, we'll...we'll carry out our plan," he said thickly.

"Ronnie, please."

"That's it, Ms. McCoy. You tell them."

Calloway answered her call before the completion of the first ring. "I'm coming out with the baby. Have medical personnel standing by. I'm bringing out three of the hostages with me."

"Only three?"

"Three."

"What about the rest?"

"I'll tell you when I get there."

She hung up on him.

As Tiel approached Sabra, the young woman was crying. "Bye-bye, sweet Katherine. My beautiful baby girl. Mommie loves you. Very much." She was bent over the child, inhaling her scent, touching her everywhere. She kissed Katherine's face several times, then turned her own into Doc's shirt and sobbed.

Tiel took the baby from Gladys, who'd been holding her because Sabra didn't have the strength. Tiel carried Katherine over to Ronnie. As the young man gazed at the baby, his eyes filled with tears. His lower lip trembled uncontrollably. He was trying so hard to be tough, and failing miserably.

"Thanks for all you've done," he said to Tiel. "I know Sabra liked having you around."

Tiel's eyes appealed to him. "I don't believe you'll do it, Ronnie. I refuse to believe you would—could—pull that trigger and end Sabra's life and yours."

He chose not to respond and instead kissed the baby's forehead. "Bye, Katherine. I love you." Then, his motions jerky and abrupt, he stepped behind the counter to release the electric door lock.

Tiel allowed the others to go ahead of her. Before stepping through the door, she glanced over her shoulder at Doc. He had eased Sabra back onto the floor, but he raised his head as though Tiel's gaze had beckoned him. Their eyes connected for only a millisecond, but, undeniably, it was a meaningful span of time and contact.

Then she slipped through the door and heard the bolt snap into place behind her.

———◆———

From out of the darkness paramedics rushed forward. Obviously, pairs of them had been pre-assigned to each hostage. Vern, Gladys, and Donna were surrounded and barraged with questions, which Gladys answered in a decidedly querulous tone.

A man and woman wearing identical scrubs and lab coats materialized in front of Tiel. The woman reached for Katherine, but Tiel didn't relinquish her just yet. "Who are you?"

"Dr. Emily Garrett." She introduced herself as chief of the neonatal unit at a Midland hospital. "This is Dr. Landry Giles, chief of obstetrics."

Tiel acknowledged the introductions, then said, "Regardless of anything you've heard to the contrary, the parents do not wish to put the child up for adoption."

Dr. Garrett's expression was as steadfast and guileless as Tiel could have hoped for. "I understand completely. We'll be waiting for the mother's arrival."

Tiel kissed the top of Katherine's head. She had a bond with this baby that she probably would never have with another human being—she had witnessed her birth, her first breath, had heard her first cry. Even so, the depth of her emotion surprised her. "Take good care of her."

"You have my word."

Dr. Garrett took the baby and ran with her toward the waiting chopper, the blades of which were already whirling and kicking up a fierce wind. Dr. Giles had to shout to make himself heard above the racket.

"How's the mother?"

"Not good." Tiel gave him a condensed version of the labor and birth, then described Sabra's present condition. "Doc's most worried about loss of blood and infection. Sabra's becoming increasingly weak. Her blood pressure is dropping, he said. Based on what I've told you, is there anything you can advise him to do?"

"Get her to the hospital."

"We're working on it," she said grimly.

The man approaching with a long and purposeful stride could only be Calloway. He was tall and slender, but even in shirtsleeves he exuded an air of authority. "Bill Calloway," he said, confirming his identity as soon as he joined her and Dr. Giles. They shook hands.

Gully hobbled up to her in his bandy-legged run. "Jesus, kid, if I don't die of a heart attack after tonight, I'll live forever."

She hugged him. "You'll outlive us all."

On the fringes of the growing group she noticed a stout man dressed in a white cowboy shirt with pearl buttons. He held a cowboy hat similar to Doc's in his hands. Before she could introduce herself to him, he was rudely elbowed aside.

"Ms. McCoy, I want to talk to you."

She recognized Russell Dendy immediately.

"How's my daughter?"

"She's dying." While the statement seemed unnecessarily harsh, Tiel was fresh out of compassion for the millionaire. Besides, if she were to make a dent in this stalemate, she must hit them hard.

Kip was standing in the background, capturing this suspenseful conference on videotape. The camera-mounted spotlight was blinding. For the first time in her career, Tiel felt an aversion for that light and the invasion of privacy it represented.

Her blunt response to Dendy's question took him aback momentarily, which enabled Calloway to draw the other man forward for an introduction. "Cole Davison, Tiel McCoy." The resemblance between Ronnie and his father was unmistakable. "How is he?" he asked anxiously.

"Resolute, Mr. Davison." Before continuing, she looked at each of the men independently. "Those young people mean what they say. They took an oath, which they intend to uphold. Now that they know Katherine is safe and receiving medical attention, there's nothing to stop them from carrying out their suicide pact." She used the words deliberately to emphasize the seriousness and urgency of the situation.

Calloway maintained his professional detachment and was the first to speak. "Sheriff Montez says this Doc is a large, brawny man. Couldn't he simply overpower Ronnie and get control of the gun?"

"And risk another casualty?" she asked rhetorically.

"Two men tried force a little while ago. It ended in bloodshed. I think I can safely nix that idea on Doc's behalf. He's been trying to persuade Ronnie to end this peaceably. He'd lose any advantage he's gained with the boy if he suddenly tried to jump him."

Calloway ran a hand through his thinning hair and watched the chopper with Dr. Garrett and the newborn lift off. "The hostages aren't at risk?" he asked.

"I don't believe so. Although there's no love lost between Ronnie and Agent Cain or the Mexican men."

They exchanged an uneasy look all around, but before Tiel could ask what it portended, Calloway said, "To summarize, Ronnie and Sabra are bartering with their own lives."

"Exactly, Mr. Calloway. I was sent to tell you that you have half an hour to get back to them."

"With what?"

"Clemency, and freedom to go on their way."

"That's impossible."

"Then you'll have two dead kids on your hands."

"You're a reasonable person, Ms. McCoy. You know I can't make that kind of blanket deal with an alleged felon."

Despair and defeat settled on her heavily. "I know, and, honestly, I appreciate the position you're in, Mr. Calloway. I'm only the messenger. I'm telling you what Ronnie told me. My gut feeling is that he means to do what he has said he will. Even if he's bluffing, Sabra is not."

She looked pointedly at Dendy. "If she can't have Ronnie, live with him freely, she's willing to take her own life. If she doesn't bleed to death first." Back to Calloway, she said, "Unfortunately for you, it's not my gut feeling that counts. The decision doesn't rest with me. It's yours to make."

"Not entirely, it isn't," Dendy declared. "I have a say in this. Calloway, for godsake, promise the boy anything. Just get my daughter out of there."

Calloway checked his wristwatch. "Half an hour," he said briskly. "Not much time, and I've got some calls to make." They turned in unison toward the van parked on the apron of the parking lot.

Gully was the first to notice that Tiel didn't fall into step with the rest of them. He turned and regarded her curiously. "Tiel?"

She was walking backward. "I'm going back."

"You aren't serious?" Gully's exclamation spoke for all of them, who were looking at her with unmitigated dismay.

"I can't abandon Sabra."

"But—"

She shook her head firmly, checking Gully's protest before it was out. Continuing to backtrack and widen the distance between them, she said, "We'll be waiting for your decision, Mr. Calloway."

Chapter 14

Tiel stood facing the door of the store for a full ninety seconds before she heard the bolt being released. As she reentered, Ronnie eyed her warily.

She dispelled his suspicion. "I'm not carrying a concealed weapon, Ronnie."

"What did Calloway say?"

"He's thinking it over. He said he has to make some phone calls."

"To who? What for?"

"I gather he doesn't have the authority to grant you clemency."

Ronnie gnawed his lower lip, which had already been so brutalized it was raw. "Okay. But why'd you come back?"

"To let you know that Katherine is in excellent hands." She told him about Dr. Emily Garrett.

"Tell Sabra. She'll want to know that."

The young mother's eyes were half closed. Her breathing was shallow. Tiel wasn't sure she was completely aware and listening, but after describing to her the neonatal specialist, Sabra whispered, "Is she nice?"

"Very. When you meet her, you'll see." Tiel glanced over at Doc, but he was taking Sabra's blood pressure, his eyebrows pulled together in the steep frown she'd come to recognize. "There's another very nice doctor waiting to take care of you. His name is Dr. Giles. You're not afraid to fly in helicopters, are you?"

"I did once. With my dad. It was okay."

"Dr. Giles is standing by to whisk you off to the hospital in Midland. Katherine will be glad to see you when you get there. She'll probably be hungry."

Sabra smiled, then her eyes closed.

By tacit agreement, Tiel and Doc retreated to their familiar posts. Seated on the floor with their backs propped against the freezer chest, legs extended in front of them, watching the second hand on the clock tick off the time limit Ronnie had imposed, it was the ideal moment for Doc to ask the question that Tiel expected from him.

"Why'd you come back?"

Even assuming that he would ask, she had no clear-cut answer prepared.

Several moments elapsed. His jaw was dark with stubble, she noticed, but it must be going on twenty-four hours since his last shave. The webwork around his eyes seemed more defined now than earlier, a distinct sign of fatigue. His clothes, like hers, were grimy and blood-stained.

Blood was a cohesive agent, she realized. It wasn't necessarily the comingling of blood from two individuals that formed an irrevocable, almost mystical, bond between them. It could be anyone's shed blood that united people.

Consider survivors of plane crashes, train wrecks, natural disasters, and terrorist attacks, who had developed lasting friendships because of the trauma they had shared. Veterans of the same war spoke a language among themselves that was incomprehensible to those who hadn't been there and experienced similar horrors. Bloodshed at the explosion in Oklahoma City, the public school shootings, and other unthinkable events had soldered former strangers together so solidly that the relationships would never be severed.

Survivors shared a common ground. Their connection was rare and unique, sometimes misinterpreted and misunderstood, but almost always unexplainable to those who hadn't encountered identical fears.

Tiel had taken so long to answer that Doc repeated his question. "Why'd you come back?"

"For Sabra," she replied. "I was the only woman left. I thought she might need me. And..."

He raised his knees, propped his forearms on them and looked at her, waiting patiently for her to complete her thought.

"And I hate to start something and not finish it. I was here when it started, so I figured I should stick around until it's over."

It wasn't quite as simple as that. Her reason for returning was more complex, but she was at a loss to explain her multilayered motivation to Doc when even to her it was unclear. Why wasn't she out there doing a live remote, taking advantage of the extraordinary insight she had on this story? Why wasn't she recording a voice track to couple with the dramatic images Kip was getting on video?

"What were you doing out here?"

Doc's question roused her from her musings. "In

Rojo Flats?" She laughed. "I was on vacation." She explained how she was en route to New Mexico when she heard of the so-called kidnaping on her car radio. "I called Gully, who assigned me to interview Cole Davison. On my way to Hera I got lost. I stopped here to use the rest room and call Gully for directions."

"That's who you were talking to when I came in?"

Tiel's gaze sharpened on him, her expression inquisitive.

He raised his shoulder in a slight shrug. "I noticed you back there on the pay phone."

"You did? Oh." Their eyes connected and held, and it was an effort for her to break that stare. "Anyway, I concluded my call and was buying snacks for the road when...who should walk in but Ronnie and Sabra."

"That's a story in itself."

"I couldn't believe my good fortune." She smiled wryly. "Be careful what you wish for."

"I am." After a beat of five, he added quietly, "Now."

This time it was she who waited him out, giving him the opportunity either to expound on his thought or to let the subject drop. He must have felt the same implied pressure from her silence that she had felt from him earlier, because he rolled his shoulders as though his burdensome reflections were resting on them.

"After I found out about Shari's affair, I wanted her to..." He faltered, began again. "I was so pissed, I wanted her to..."

"Suffer."

"Yeah."

The long sigh he released around the word evinced his relief over finally getting the confession off his chest. Confidences wouldn't come easily to a man like him who had dealt in life-and-death situations on a daily basis. To have the courage and tenacity to battle such a seemingly omnipotent enemy as cancer, there was surely a generous degree of the god complex in Bradley Stanwick's makeup. Vulnerability, any sign of weakness, was incompatible with that personality trait. No, beyond incompatible. Intolerable.

Tiel was flattered that he had confessed a weakness, had revealed to her even a glimpse of this all-too-human aspect of himself. She supposed traumatic situations were good for that, too. Like a deathbed confession, he might be thinking this was the last chance he would have to unburden himself of the guilt he had carried over his wife's terminal illness.

"Her cancer wasn't punishment for her adultery," she argued gently. "It certainly wasn't your revenge."

"I know. Rationally and reasonably I know that. But when she was going through the worst of it—and, believe me, it was sheer hell—that's what I thought about. That I had subconsciously wished it on her."

"So now you're punishing yourself with this self-imposed banishment from your profession."

He fired back, "And you're not?"

"What?"

"Punishing yourself because your husband got killed. You're doing the work of two people to make up for the industry loss created when he died."

"That's ridiculous!"

"Is it?"

"Yes. I work hard because I love it."

"But you'll never be able to do enough, will you?"

An angry retort died on her lips. She had never examined the psychology behind her ambition. She had never *allowed* herself to examine it. But now that she'd been confronted with this hypothesis, she had to admit that it had merit. The ambition had always been there. She had been born with a type-A personality, was always an overachiever.

But not to the degree of the last few years. She pursued goals with a vengeance and took perceived failures hard. She worked to the exclusion of everything else. It wasn't a matter of her career taking precedence over other areas of her life; it *was* her life. Was her mad, singular desire to succeed a self-inflicted penance for those few ill-chosen words spoken in the heat of anger? Was guilt her propellant?

They lapsed into silence, each lost in his own troubling thoughts, grappling with the personal demons they'd been forced to acknowledge.

"Where in New Mexico?"

"What?" Tiel turned to him. "Oh, my destination? Angel Fire."

"Heard of it. Never been there."

"Mountain air and clear streams. Aspen trees. They'd be green now, not gold, but I hear it's beautiful."

"You hear? You haven't been there either?"

She shook her head. "A friend was lending me her condo for the week."

"You'd be there by now, all tucked in. Too bad you placed that first call to Gully."

"I don't know, Doc." She glanced at Sabra, then looked at him. Closely. Taking in every nuance of his rugged face. Plumbing the depths of his eyes. "I wouldn't have missed this for the world."

The urge to touch him was almost irresistible. She did resist, but she didn't break eye contact. It lasted a long time, while her heart thudded hard and heavily against her ribs and her senses hummed with a keen, sweet awareness of him.

She actually jumped when the telephone rang.

Clumsily she scrambled to her feet, and so did Doc.

Ronnie grabbed the receiver. "Mr. Calloway?"

He listened for what seemed to Tiel an eternity. Again she curbed the impulse to touch Doc. She wanted to take his hand and hold on to it tightly, as people are wont to do when waiting to hear life-altering news.

Finally Ronnie turned to them and placed the earpiece against his chest. "Calloway says he's got the district attorney of Tarrant County, and whatever this county is, plus a judge, himself, and both sets of parents, agreed to meet and hammer this thing out. He says if I admit to wrongdoing and submit to counseling, maybe I'll get probation and not have to go to jail. Maybe."

Tiel nearly collapsed with relief. A small laugh bubbled from her throat. "That's great!"

"It's a good deal, Ronnie. If I were you, I'd grab it," Doc told him.

"Sabra, is that okay with you?"

When she didn't respond, Doc nearly knocked Tiel off her feet as he brushed past her and knelt beside the girl. "She's unconscious."

"Oh, God," Ronnie cried. "Is she dead?"

"No, but she's got to get help, son. And I mean fast."

Tiel left Sabra in Doc's care and moved toward Ronnie. She was afraid that in his despair, he might yet turn the pistol on himself. "Tell Calloway you agree to the terms. I'm going to cut the tape binding them," she said, gesturing to Cain, Juan, and Two. "Okay?"

Ronnie was transfixed by the sight of Doc lifting Sabra into his arms. Blood immediately saturated his clothes. "Oh, Jesus, oh, God, what've I done?"

"Save the regrets for later, Ronnie," Doc said in a stern voice. "Tell Calloway we're coming out."

The dazed young man began mumbling into the mouthpiece. Tiel quickly retrieved the scissors they'd used earlier and knelt down beside Cain. She sawed through the tape around his ankles. "What about my hands?" His tongue seemed thick. The man probably had two concussions.

"When you get outside." She still didn't trust him not to try and be a hero.

His eyes narrowed to slits. "You're in deep shit, lady."

"Usually," Tiel quipped, and moved to the Mexican men.

Juan was enduring his leg wound stoically, but she could feel resentment emanating from him like heat from a furnace. Keeping as much distance as possible between him and herself, she cut the tape around his ankles. It took some effort. Vern had done an excellent job.

She felt even more aversion for the one she'd nicknamed Two. His dark eyes roved over her with unconcealed malevolence and an intentionally demeaning, sexual suggestiveness that made her feel in even more need of a shower.

That chore completed, she said, "Doc, go first," and motioned him toward the door. "Right, Ronnie?"

"Right, right. Get Sabra to someone who can help her, Doc."

Tiel moved to the door and held it open for him. Sabra looked like a faded rag doll in his arms. She looked dead. Ronnie lovingly touched her hair, her cheek. When she didn't respond, he moaned.

"Hang in there, Ronnie, she's alive," Doc assured him. "She'll be okay."

"Dr. Giles," Tiel told Doc as he moved past with the girl.

"Got it."

In a blink, he was gone, running across the parking lot carrying the unconscious girl.

"You next," Ronnie said to Tiel.

She shook her head. "I'm staying with you. We'll go out together."

"You don't trust them?" he asked in a voice made high and thin by fright. "You think Calloway will try and pull something?"

"I don't trust *them*." She hitched her head back toward the other three hostages. "Let them go first."

He contemplated that, but only for an instant. "Okay. You. Cain. Go."

The vanquished FBI agent skulked past them. Because his hands were still bound, Tiel once again held the door open. More injurious than the two clouts to his head was the blow his pride had sustained. No doubt he dreaded facing his fellow agents, particularly Calloway.

Ronnie waited until Cain had been swallowed up by a crowd of paramedics and officials before he motioned Juan and Two toward the door. "You next."

After trying twice to escape, they now seemed reluctant to leave. They shuffled forward, muttering to one another in Spanish.

"Come on," Tiel said, impatiently motioning them through the door. She was frantic to know how Sabra was faring.

Juan went first, limping noticeably. He hesitated on the threshold, his eyes darting to various points on the parking lot. Two, she noticed, was practically on Juan's heels, standing belly to butt as though using the other man as a shield. They stepped through the door.

Tiel had turned to speak to Ronnie when suddenly the front of the store was seared with blinding light. The SWAT team, looking like black beetles, came scurrying from every conceivable hiding place. Their number amazed her. She hadn't seen a third of them when she'd gone out to confer with Calloway.

Ronnie cursed and ducked behind the counter. Tiel screamed, but from outrage, not fear. She was too livid to be afraid.

Oddly, however, the tactical officers surrounded Juan and Two, ordering them to lie facedown on the ground. The injured Juan had no choice but to comply. He practically crumpled.

Heedless of the warnings shouted at him, Two took off at a dead run but was almost immediately tackled and knocked to the concrete. Before Tiel could assimilate what had happened, it was over. The two men were shackled and dragged away by the SWAT team.

The lights went out as suddenly as they'd come on.

"Ronnie?" His name was bellowed through a bullhorn. "Ronnie? Ms. McCoy?" It was Calloway.

"Don't be alarmed. You've been in the company of some very dangerous men. We saw them on the videotape and recognized them. They're wanted by the authorities here and in Mexico. That's why they were so eager to escape. But they're in our custody now. It's safe for you to come out."

Far from being calmed by this information, Tiel was furious. How dare they not warn her of the potential danger! But she couldn't vent her anger now. She would take it up with Calloway and company later.

With as much composure as she could muster, she said to Ronnie, "You heard him. Everything's okay. The lights, the SWAT team had nothing to do with you. Let's go."

He still looked afraid and uncertain. In any case, he didn't move from behind the counter.

God, please don't let me make a deadly mistake now, Tiel prayed. She couldn't push him too hard, but she had to push hard enough to get him moving.

"I think it would be best if you left the pistols here, don't you? Lay them there on the counter. Then you can walk out with your hands up, and they'll know that you're sincere in wanting to work things out." He didn't move. "Right?"

He looked tired, depleted, defeated. *No, no, not defeated,* she corrected. If he looked upon this as a defeat, he might not leave. He might take what would seem to him the easier way out.

"You did an exceptionally brave thing, Ronnie," she said conversationally. "Standing up to Russell Dendy. The FBI. You've won. What you and Sabra wanted all along was an audience, someone to listen and play fair with you. And you've got them to agree to do just that. That's quite an achievement."

His eyes strayed to her. She smiled, hoping it didn't look as phony and wooden as it felt—indeed, as it was. "Set the guns down and let's go. I'll hold your hand if you like."

"No. No. I'll go out by myself." He placed the two pistols on the counter, and as he wiped his damp palms on the legs of his jeans, Tiel exhaled the breath she'd been holding.

"Go ahead. I'm right behind you."

She hesitated, worried about the handguns, which were still within his reach. Was his seeming compliance a trick? "Okay. I'm going. Coming?"

He licked his bruised lips. "Yeah."

Nervously she turned toward the door, opened it, and stepped through. The sky was no longer black, she noticed, but dark gray, so that the silhouettes of all the vehicles and people showed up against it. The air was already hot and dry. There was a light wind, carrying sand that abraded her skin as it blew across her.

She took a few steps before glancing back. Ronnie had his hand on the door, ready to push it open. There was no sign of a weapon in his hand. *Don't do anything harmful now, Ronnie. You're home free.*

Ahead, waiting for her, she could make out Calloway. Mr. Davison. Gully. Sheriff Montez.

And Doc. He was there. Standing a little apart from the others. Tall. Broad-shouldered. Hair lifting in the wind.

From the corner of her eye she saw the SWAT team herding Two into the back of a van under heavy guard. The door was slammed closed and the van sped from the parking lot with a screech of tires. Juan had been confined to a gurney, where paramedics were tending to him.

Tiel's glance had just moved past him when she did a double take. He began wrestling against the paramedic trying to insert an IV needle into the back of his shackled hand. Like a madman in a straightjacket, he twisted his body, his head, his arms. His mouth was moving, forming words, and she wondered why she found that so puzzling.

Then she realized that the words he was shouting were in English.

But he didn't speak English, she thought stupidly. Only Spanish.

Furthermore, the words made no sense because he was yelling at the top of his lungs. "He's got a rifle! There! Somebody! Oh, Christ, no!"

The words registered with Tiel a split second before Juan sprang off the gurney, executed a horizontal body dive off the concrete, and went airborne. He launched himself into the man, his shoulder landing hard against the other's torso and knocking him to the ground.

But not before Russell Dendy got off a clean shot with a deer rifle.

Tiel heard the shattering sound and spun around to see the door of the convenience store raining glass onto Ronnie's prone form. She didn't remember later if she screamed or not. She didn't remember later crossing the distance back to the entrance of the store at a full-out run, or dropping to her hands and knees despite the glass.

She did recall hearing Juan shout—to save his life— "Martinez, undercover Treasury agent! Martinez, Treasury agent, working undercover!"

Chapter 15

The antiseptic the paramedic was dabbing onto her hands and knees made them sting. The broken glass had sliced through the fabric of her trousers, which had been cut off above her knees.

Tiel hadn't noticed the cuts at all until the paramedic began removing splinters of glass with tiny tweezers. Only then had they begun to hurt. The pain wasn't significant, however. She was more interested in what was going on around her than in the superficial wounds she had sustained.

Seated on a gurney—she had refused to climb inside the ambulance—she tried to see around the woman who was treating her. It was a chaotic scene. In the pale dawn, the lights of a dozen police and emergency vehicles created a dizzying kaleidoscope of flashing, colored lights. Medical personnel, those who hadn't rushed to Ronnie's aid, were seeing to her, Treasury Agent Martinez, and Cain.

The media had been denied access to the immediate

area, but news helicopters buzzed overhead like brute insects. Parked on a mesa overlooking the depression known as Rojo Flats was a convoy of television vans. The satellite dishes mounted on their roofs reflected the new sun.

Ordinarily this would be the kind of scene on which Tiel McCoy thrived. She would be in her element. But the customary rush of adrenaline just hadn't been there when she stared into the lens of the video camera to do her live report.

She had tried to work up her usual level of enthusiasm, but she knew it was lacking and only hoped that the viewing audience wouldn't notice, or that if they did that they would assign her lack of verve to the ordeal she had endured.

The report certainly had a dramatic backdrop. She had shouted into her microphone as the CareFlight helicopter lifted off, bearing Ronnie Davison to the nearest emergency center, where a trauma team was standing by to treat the gunshot wound in his chest. The fierce winds created by the whirling blades whipped sand into her eyes. It was the blowing sand to which she attributed her unprofessional tears.

As soon as she concluded her ad-libbed summary of the events that had transpired over the past six hours, she listlessly passed the wireless mike back to Kip, who kissed her cheek, said, "Terrific," then rushed off to shoot more B-roll, taking advantage of the access he had to the scene because of his association with her.

Only after finishing that piece of business had she consented to having her bleeding palms and knees examined. Now, speaking to the paramedic, she said, "You must know something."

"I'm sorry, Ms. McCoy. I don't."

"Or you aren't telling."

The woman gave her a retiring look. "I don't know." She recapped the bottle of antiseptic. "You really should go to the hospital and let someone look at these hands under better light. There might be glass slivers—"

"There aren't. I'm fine." She jumped off the gurney. Her knees were becoming sore and stiff from the multiple cuts, but she hid her grimace from the paramedic. "Thank you."

"Tiel, you okay?" Gully came huffing up to her. "These sumbitches wouldn't let me past till you got those hands and knees seen to. The video looks great, kid. Best you've ever done. If this doesn't get you the *Nine Live* spot, then life ain't fair and I'm gonna quit the TV business myself."

"Have you heard anything about Ronnie's condition?"

"Not a thing."

"Sabra?"

"Nothing. Not since the cowboy turned her over to that Dr. Giles and they took her off in the chopper."

"Speaking of Doc, is he around?"

Gully didn't hear her. He was shaking his head and muttering, "Wish they had given me a crack at Dendy. A couple of minutes with me and he'd've been hating life."

"I assume he's under arrest."

"The sheriff had three deputies—meanest-looking cusses I've ever seen—haul his ass off to jail."

Even though she had seen it with her own eyes, she still found it impossible to believe that Dendy had shot Ronnie Davison. She expressed her dismay to Gully. "I don't understand how that could have happened."

"Nobody was paying him any attention. He had put

on a good show for Calloway. Crying, wringing his hands. Admitted that he'd mishandled things. He led us to believe that he had seen the error of his ways, that all was forgiven, and that he only wanted Sabra to be safe. The lying bastard."

Tiel's pent-up emotions boiled to the surface, and she began to cry. "It's my fault, Gully. I promised Ronnie it would be safe for him to come out, that if he surrendered, he wouldn't be hurt."

"That's what we all promised him, Ms. McCoy."

She turned toward the familiar voice, her tears drying instantly. "I'm very put out with you, Agent Calloway."

"As your colleague just explained, I fell for Dendy's act of contrition. Nobody knew he had brought a deer rifle with him."

"Not just that. You could have warned me about that Huerta character when I brought the baby out."

"And if you'd known who he was, what would you have done?"

What would she have done? She didn't know, but somehow that seemed irrelevant. She asked, "Did you know Martinez was a Treasury agent?"

Calloway looked chagrined. "No. We assumed he was one of Huerta's henchmen."

Remembering how the wounded, shackled man had flung himself at Dendy, she remarked, "He did an awfully brave thing. Not only did he blow his cover, but he also risked his life. If any of the other officers had reacted more quickly..." She shuddered to think of the young man's body being riddled with bullets from fellow officers' guns.

"I've thought of that," Calloway admitted grimly. "He'd like to talk to you."

"Me?"

"Are you up to it?"

Calloway led her to another ambulance, apprising her along the way of Martinez's condition. "The bullet went straight through his leg without nicking a bone or an artery. Twice tonight he got lucky." He assisted her into the back of the ambulance.

The temporary dressing Doc had put on Martinez's thigh had been replaced by a sterile gauze bandage. The bloody T-shirt had been added to the pile of other infectious waste materials about to be discarded. Seeing it caused Tiel's heart to constrict. She recalled seeing Doc's hands fashioning the crude bandage for the wound he had inflicted.

Martinez was hooked up to an IV and was also getting a transfusion of blood. But his eyes were clear. "Ms. McCoy."

"Agent Martinez. You're very good at your job. You had us all fooled."

He smiled, showing the very straight white teeth she had noticed before. "That's the goal of an undercover operative. Thank God Huerta was also fooled. I've been a member of his organization since last summer. A truckload of people came across the border last night."

"It was intercepted about an hour ago," Calloway informed them. "As usual, the conditions inside were deplorable. The people locked in were actually grateful for being taken into custody. They considered it a rescue."

"Huerta and I were on our way to make the sale to a wheat farmer up in Kansas. Huerta was to be arrested as soon as the transaction went down. We stopped here to get a snack."

He shrugged, as though to say they knew the rest.

"I'm just glad that neither of us went into that store armed. We'd left our weapons in the car—something that never happens. It was a twist of fate, or divine intervention, whatever. If Huerta had been carrying, it would've got real ugly real soon."

"Will you be in danger of reprisal?"

Again he flashed a smile. "I'm trusting the department to make me disappear. If you ever see me again, you probably won't recognize me."

"I see. One more question, why did you try and take the baby?"

"Huerta wanted to rush Ronnie, overpower him. I volunteered to distract everyone by grabbing the baby. Actually, I was afraid he'd do something to the child. That was the only way I knew to protect her."

Tiel shivered at the thought of what might have been. "You seemed particularly hostile toward Cain."

"He recognized me," Martinez exclaimed. "We'd worked a case together a couple years ago. He didn't have the good sense to keep his trap shut. Several times he nearly blew it for me. I had to shut him up." Looking at Calloway, he added, "I think he needs a refresher course at Quantico."

Tiel hid her smile. "We have you to thank for several acts of bravery, Mr. Martinez. I'm sorry you got shot for your effort."

"That guy—Doc—did what he had to do. If the situation had been reversed, I'd have done the same. I'd like to tell him I don't hold a grudge."

Calloway said, "He's already left."

Hiding her disappointment and despite the small cuts on her palm, Tiel shook Martinez's hand and wished him well, then was helped down out of the ambulance, where Gully was smoking a cigarette while waiting. As the ambulance pulled away, Gladys and Vern joined them.

Apparently they had returned to their RV, because they were wearing different clothes, smelled of soap, and were looking as spry and alert as though they'd just returned from a two-week visit to a health spa. Tiel hugged them in turn.

"We couldn't leave without giving you our address and getting your promise to stay in touch." Gladys handed her a slip of paper on which was written an address in Florida.

"I promise. Are you continuing the honeymoon from here?"

"After a stop in Louisiana to see my son and grand-children," Vern said.

"Who are without a doubt the five most ornery little bastards on earth."

"Now, Gladys."

"I'm only telling it like it is, Vern. They're heathens and you know it." Then her demeanor changed. She blotted away the tears that suddenly appeared in her eyes. "I just hope those two young people come through this. I'll be worried sick until I hear that they're all right."

"So will I." Tiel squeezed Gladys's small hand.

Vern said, "We had to give our statements to the sheriff, then to the FBI agents. We told them you couldn't help hitting that Cain with the chili on account of he was such an idiot."

Gully snickered. Calloway tensed, but he let the criticism go without comment.

"Donna's hogging the TV cameras," Gladys said with pique. "To hear her tell it, she was a heroine."

Vern reached into his tote bag, removed a small

videocassette, and pressed it into Tiel's hand. "Don't forget this," he whispered.

Actually, she had forgotten the camcorder tape.

Gladys said, "We sneaked back into the store to get it."

"Thank you. For everything." Tiel got emotional again when they said their final farewell and headed for their RV.

"Honeymoon?" Gully asked as they moved away.

"They were terrific. I'm going to miss them."

He looked at her strangely. "Are you okay?"

"Yes. Why?"

"Because you're acting sorta weird."

"I've been up all night." Straightening her shoulders and adopting the demeanor she assumed when cameras were about to roll, she turned to Calloway. "I suppose you have a lot of questions for me."

In the van, Calloway plied her with coffee and breakfast burritos donated by the ladies' auxiliary of the First Baptist Church. It took over an hour for him to get from her all the information he required.

"I think that's it for now, Ms. McCoy, although we'll probably have some follow-up questions."

"I understand."

"And it wouldn't surprise me if the respective DAs ask you to attend when we convene to discuss the charges against Ronnie Davison."

"*If* you convene," she said softly.

The FBI agent looked away, and Tiel realized he bore a large measure of guilt over what had happened. Perhaps even more than she. He admitted to being duped by Russell Dendy's playacting. He hadn't noticed Dendy returning to the private charter helicopter he had arrived in and retrieving a deer rifle from it. If the unthinkable happened and Ronnie died, Calloway would have much to account for.

"Have you received any update on Ronnie's condition?"

"No," Calloway replied. "All I know is that he was alive when they put him in the chopper. I've heard nothing further. The baby is fine. Sabra is listed in poor condition, which is better than I had hoped for. She's received several units of blood. Her mother is with her."

"I haven't seen Mr. Cole Davison."

"They let him accompany Ronnie in the helicopter. He was...well, you can imagine."

They were quiet for a moment, impervious to the activity of the other agents, who were busy with the "mopping up." Eventually Calloway signaled her out of her chair and escorted her outside, where the morning was now full blown.

"Good-bye, Mr. Calloway."

"Ms. McCoy?" Having started to walk away, she turned back. Special Agent Calloway looked slightly ill at ease with what he was about to say. "This was a terrible ordeal for you, I'm sure. But I'm glad we had someone in there who is as level-headed as you. You helped keep everyone sane and acted with remarkable composure."

"I'm not remarkable, Mr. Calloway. Bossy maybe," she said with a wan smile. "If it hadn't been for Doc—" She tilted her head inquisitively. "Did he give you his statement?"

"Sheriff Montez took his."

He motioned her toward the sheriff, whom she hadn't noticed leaning against the side of the van in the shade. He tipped his wide-brimmed hat and ambled toward her, but ignored her unspoken question about Doc.

"Our mayor has offered to put you up at the local motel. It's not the Ritz," he warned with a chuckle. "But you're welcome to stay as long as you like."

"Thank you, but I'm returning to Dallas."

"Not right now you're not." Gully had joined them, and with him was Kip. "We're going back in the chopper and deliver this tape to the editor so she can start putting the piece together."

"I'll go too, and send someone back for my car."

He was shaking his head before Tiel finished speaking. "Not enough room for more than two passengers, and I gotta get back. No telling what that freak with the rings in his eyebrow has done to my newsroom. You take the mayor up on his kind offer. We'll send the chopper for you later, along with an intern to drive your car back to Dallas. Besides, you stink. A shower wouldn't hurt."

"You really know how to turn on the charm when you have to, Gully."

It seemed the matter was settled, and she was too exhausted to put up much of a fight. They specified a time and place for her to meet the helicopter, and Sheriff Montez promised to have her there. Gully and Kip said their good-byes and hustled off toward the waiting chopper with the station's call letters painted on the sides.

Calloway extended his hand. "Good luck to you, Ms. McCoy."

"And to you." She shook hands with him, but when he would have withdrawn, she detained him. "You said you were glad it was me who was in there," she said, nodding in the direction of the store. "I'm glad it was you out here, Mr. Calloway." And she meant it. They'd been very lucky to have him as the agent in charge of such a delicate situation. Another might not have handled it with the sensitivity he had shown.

The implied compliment seemed to embarrass him. "Thank you," he said briskly, then turned and reentered the van.

Sheriff Montez retrieved her bags from her car and placed them in the back seat of his squad car. She protested his chauffeuring her. "I can drive myself, Sheriff."

"No need. You're so tuckered out, I'd be afraid you'd fall asleep at the wheel. If you're worried about your car, I'll send a deputy over for it. We'll keep it parked at our office where we can keep an eye on it."

Surprisingly, she found it a welcome change to relinquish control and to not have to make any mind-taxing decisions. "Thank you."

It was a short trip to the motel. Six rooms were lined up along a covered breezeway that provided a hair's-breadth of shade. All the doors were painted UT orange.

"No need to check in. You're the only guest." Montez slid from behind the steering wheel and came around to assist her out.

He had the room key and used it to open the door. The air conditioner had already been turned on. The window unit hummed loudly and one of its internal parts clanked intermittently, but these were friendly sounds. A vase of sunflowers and a basket filled with fresh fruit and baked goods wrapped in pink plastic had been placed on the room's one small table.

"The Catholic ladies weren't about to be outdone by the Baptists," he told her.

"You've all been very kind."

"Not at all, Ms. McCoy. Weren't for you, it could've

gone a lot worse. None of us wanted Rojo Flats to be put on the map by something like a massacre." He touched the brim of his hat as he backed out, pulling the door closed behind him. "You want anything, call the desk. Otherwise nobody'll bother you. Rest well. I'll be back for you later."

Ordinarily the first thing Tiel did upon entering a room was switch on the television set. She was a news junkie. Whether or not she was actually watching the screen, she was always tuned to a twenty-four-hour news station. She fell asleep to it, and woke up to it.

Now, she moved past the TV set without even noticing it and carried her toiletry bag with her into the minuscule bathroom. The shower was barely large enough to turn around in, but the water was hot and there was plenty of it. Standing beneath the steaming spray, she let it pound against her skull before shampooing. She lathered lavishly with her imported soap sold exclusively at Neiman's. She shaved her legs, avoiding the lacerations on her knees. She used her hair dryer only long enough to blow out most of the water, then bent over the sink to brush her teeth.

All of which felt wonderful.

So why did she feel so lousy?

She had just filed the most important story of her career. *Nine Live* was as good as hers now. Gully had said so. She should be dancing on the ceiling. Instead her limbs felt as though they weighed a thousand pounds apiece. Where was the fizzy high she derived from a good news story? Her spirit was as flat as three-day-old champagne.

Sleep deprivation. That was it. Once she had napped for several hours, she would be right as rain. Her old self. Recharged and ready.

Back in the bedroom, she took a tank top and briefs from her suitcase and put them on, set her travel alarm clock, then turned down the bed. The sheets looked soft and inviting. It occurred to her that her knees and palms might bleed on them, but she was beyond caring.

When she heard the knock, she took it for another ping in the air conditioner's mechanism. But when it was followed by a second, she moved to the door and pulled it open.

Chapter 16

He stepped inside, closed the door behind him, removed his sunglasses and hat, and set them on the table beside the untouched basket of goodies the ladies from the Catholic church had prepared for her.

He smelled of sunshine and soap; he was freshly shaved. He had on clean but well-worn Levi's and a plain white shirt, a western tooled-leather belt, and cowboy boots.

If a team of mustangs had been pulling Tiel in the opposite direction, they couldn't have stopped her from throwing herself against him. Or maybe he reached for her. Afterward, she didn't recall who moved first. And anyway, who initiated it was unimportant.

All that mattered was that he drew her into an all-encompassing embrace. Her body was flush with his, and they held each other tightly. Her brimming tears flowed freely and were absorbed by the cloth of his shirt. He covered the back of her head with his wide hand and pressed her face into his chest to cushion the sobs that issued from her in short, noisy bursts.

"Did he die? Are you here to tell me that Ronnie is dead?"

"No, that's not why I'm here. I don't know any news about Ronnie."

"I guess that's good."

"I guess."

"I couldn't believe it, Doc. That sound. That horrible, deafening sound. Then to see him lying there so still, amidst all that glass and blood. More blood."

"Shh."

Comforting words were whispered across her hairline, along her temple. Then the words ceased, and only his breath, his lips, drifted over her brow, touching her damp eyelids. Tiel raised her head and looked at him through tearful eyes. Reaching up to touch his face, she made a small sound of want, which he echoed.

A heartbeat later, his lips were on hers. Insistent and hungry, they rubbed hers apart. Their tongues flirted, stroked, before his dominated. It claimed and explored her mouth. Tiel's hands met at the back of his neck. She threaded her fingers up through his hair and submitted to his kiss, which was symbolically, blatantly sexual.

As though boosted by a powerful stimulant, her senses quickened. Each sensory receptor was sharpened to a fine point. She had never felt more alive, yet she was also a little afraid. Like a child at her first carnival, she was dazzled and dazed by the sensual onslaught, enthralled by it, overwhelmed by it, apprehensive of it, and yet eager to experience it.

His belt buckle gouged her tummy, but it wasn't an unpleasant sensation. The cold metal turned warm against the strip of bare skin between the hem of her tank top and her bikini line. Strong and confident, his hands settled on her lower back and pulled her closer.

He kissed his way down her throat. She angled her head to one side, and he feathered her earlobe with his breath, his tongue. Following the course of her head, she turned her body slowly, enabling him to kiss the side of her neck, her shoulder. Lifting her hair, he kissed her nape. The touch of his mouth there sent shivers of delight up her spine.

With her back to him now, she leaned against his wide chest while his hands smoothed over her front. He pressed her breasts beneath his palms, cupped them, reshaped them, before his hands continued down to her rib cage—which he was almost able to encase. At her hipbones, his hands rested.

Tingling with arousal, her movements against him were feline, shameless, inviting. He responded by slipping his hand into the front of her briefs, down, down deep into the vee of her thighs.

When he found her center, she murmured his name, turned her head, and sought his lips with hers.

They kissed while his fingers continued to caress, separate, penetrate. She came up on tiptoes, her body arching outward, straining toward his hand, until her shoulder blades were propped against his collarbone and her head was grinding into his shoulder.

She placed her hand over his, urging his fingers higher. But that still wasn't good enough. She wanted to be close to him. As close as she could be . . . and she wasn't nearly close enough.

Turning suddenly, she molded herself to his front. The sound that rumbled from his chest was low, animalistic, arousing. He palmed her bottom and lifted her against his middle. They fit like two pieces of a puzzle.

Perfectly. Snugly. Breathtakingly. Tiel raised one leg and rested it on his hip. As they kissed lustily, he stroked the underside of her thigh.

Then he carried her to the bed. It was only a distance of a few steps, but to Tiel it seemed to take forever before she felt him stretched out alongside her. She readjusted her body beneath his weight.

He pushed his fingers into her hair and held it off her face. His eyes, practically liquid with desire, seemed to pour over her features. "I don't know what you like." His voice was raspy. Even more so than usual. She wished it were tangible so she could feel it abrading her skin like the sand that had blown across her earlier.

Her fingertip traced the shape of his eyebrow, followed the length of his straight, narrow nose, outlined his lips. "I like you."

"What do you want me to do?"

For one dreadful moment, she feared she would lapse into another crying jag. Emotion made her chest and throat tight, but she managed to contain it. "Convince me I'm alive, Doc."

He began by removing her tank top and lowering his mouth to her breasts. He kissed them in turn, but lightly, teasingly, and he continued sipping at them until they were ready, and then he applied his tongue. Watching this was an incredible turn-on. She began to feel increasingly restless and hot. Pressure gathered in the lower part of her body.

Then his lips closed around her hard nipple. The silky heat, the tugging motion of his mouth, felt erotic and empowering. She couldn't keep her hips and legs still, and when her knee nudged his crotch, then stayed to prod lightly the fullness there, he grunted with a mix of pleasure and pain.

Suddenly he was off the bed. He undressed hastily. His chest had just the right amount of hair. His skin was taut. Muscles were well defined, but not grotesquely so. His belly was flat. His penis jutted aggressively from the juncture of tapering hips and strong thighs.

Just as he placed one knee on the bed, Tiel sat up. Her fingertips followed the trail of silky hair that bisected his belly down to the fan of denser growth. The shaft was warm, hard, alive; the tip velvety in texture. Without a single nod toward shyness, he allowed her to study him.

Then she wrapped her arms around his hips and hugged him close, so that her head was pressed to his lower chest and his sex was nestled between her breasts. It felt delicious.

But after a moment, he groaned, "Tiel…"

Gently he eased her back onto the bed. He leaned over her and removed her underpants. He paused for a moment, his eyes focused on her with frank interest. Then he bent down and kissed her just above the line of her pubic hair. It was a lazy, sexy, wet kiss that prompted her to reach for him with unabashed longing.

He stretched out on top of her. Her thighs parted naturally. He slid his arms beneath her back and hugged her to him.

And then he entered her.

———◆———

They were twined together naked, without even the benefit of the bedsheet to cover them. The air conditioner was blasting cold air into the small room, but their skin was radiating heat.

Tiel actually felt feverish. She lay sprawled atop him,

her head on his chest, one arm flung over his waist, one knee securely lodged in his crotch. He was breathing evenly and contentedly, idly stroking her hair.

"I thought I had hurt you."

"Hurt me?" she mumbled.

"You cried out."

Yes. At his initial thrust. She remembered now. She turned her head into his chest and nuzzled him. "Because it felt so good."

His arms tightened around her. "To me too. That thing you do—"

"What thing?"

"That thing."

"I don't do a thing."

He opened his eyes and smiled. "Yeah you do."

"I do?"

"Hmm. And it's bloody great."

Blushing, she returned her cheek to his chest. "Well, thanks."

"The pleasure was mine."

"I'm exhausted."

"So am I."

"But I don't want to sleep."

"Me either."

Several moments passed, a time of sweet reflection. Eventually Tiel stacked her hands on his sternum and propped her chin on them. "Doc?"

"Hmm."

"Are you asleep? Is it all right if I ask you something?"

"Go ahead."

"What are we doing?"

He opened only one eye to look at her. "Do you want the scientific nomenclature, the polite phraseology, or will twenty-first-century vernacular do?"

She frowned at his teasing. "I meant—"

"I know what you meant." The second eye came open, and he tilted his head on the pillow to look at her from a better angle. "Just what you said earlier, Tiel. We're convincing each other that we're alive. It's not all that uncommon for people to want sex after a life-threatening experience. Or after any reminder of their mortality, a funeral for instance. Sex is the quintessential affirmation that you're alive."

"Really? Well that's the most fan-fucking-tastic assertion of the survival instinct I've ever experienced." He chuckled. But Tiel grew quiet, introspective. She blew softly against the chest hairs brushing her lips. "Is that all it was?"

He placed his finger beneath her chin and lifted it until she was looking at him again. "Anything between us would be complicated, Tiel."

"Are you still in love with Shari?"

"I love the good memories of her. I also hate the painful ones. But, if you're suggesting that I'm fixated on her ghost, let me assure you that I'm not. My relationship with her—good, bad, or indifferent—wouldn't prevent me from having another."

"You'd marry again?"

"I'd want to. If I loved the woman, I would want to make a life together, and to me that means marriage." After a moment, he asked, "What about your memories of John Malone?"

"Like yours, bittersweet. We had almost a fairy-tale romance. Probably married too soon, aglow with passion, before we really knew one another. If he hadn't died, who knows? Career paths might eventually have led us in different and irreconcilable directions."

"As it is, he'll remain in your memory as the martyred Prince Charming."

"No, Doc. My memory isn't clinging to a flawless ghost either."

"What about that Joe?"

"That Joe is married," she reminded him.

"But if he weren't?"

She thought about Joseph Marcus a moment, then shook her head. "We probably would have had a thing going for a while, and then it would have fizzled. He was a diversion, not an affair of the heart. Nothing serious, I assure you. I can barely remember him."

She levered herself up and combed her hands down his chest. "You, on the other hand, I'll remember. You look exactly as I imagined you would."

"You imagined me naked?"

"I confess."

"When?"

"When you first came into the store, I think. In the back of my mind, I was thinking, 'Whoa. He's yummy.' "

"I'm yummy?"

"Very yummy."

"Why, thank you, ma'am," he said, speaking in an exaggerated drawl. Eyes moving to her breasts, he added, "You're right tasty-looking yourself."

"Oh, I'll bet you say that to all the girls who straddle your lap."

Smiling, he reached for a strand of her hair and rubbed it between his fingers. Gradually his smile relaxed, and when he spoke, his tone was more serious.

"We've been through a lot together, Tiel. A birth. A near-death. Tense hours of not knowing how it was going to play out. Trauma like that does something to people. It binds them."

His words echoed her earlier thoughts on the subject. But it wasn't very flattering that he ascribed their attraction solely to trauma, or that he could mitigate carnal desire with such a pragmatic, scientific explanation.

What if they'd met at a cocktail party last night? There would have been no sparks, no heat, and they wouldn't be in bed together now. Essentially that's what he was saying. If this meant nothing more to him than illustrating a psychological phenomenon, there was no sense in prolonging the inevitable good-bye.

Congratulations, Doc. You're my first—and probably last— one-night stand. One-morning stand.

She moved to get up, but he used her motion to pull her fully atop him, so that they were belly to belly and her legs were lying between his.

"In spite of the danger to us—to everyone inside the store—I had periodic and incredibly vivid fantasies of this."

She found enough voice to say, "Of this?"

His hands smoothed down her back, over her ass, and as far as they could reach along the backs of her thighs. "Of you."

He levered up his shoulders in order to kiss her. At first the kiss was slow and methodical, his tongue leisurely stroking her mouth while his hands continued sliding up and down her back from shoulders to thighs.

She felt like purring. In fact she did. When he felt the vibration of it, the kiss intensified. His hands covered her bottom and held her tightly against his erection. Provocatively, she rocked against it. He hissed a swear word, making it sound erotic. He slid his hands down the backs of her thighs and separated them.

Then he was inside her again, a full, heavy, desired pressure. Filling more than her body. Filling an unac-

knowledged need she'd had for a very long time. Giving
her more than immense pleasure. Giving her a sense of
fulfillment and purpose that even her finest work had
failed to provide.

They moved in perfect rhythm. She couldn't get as
deeply into him as she wanted, and he must have felt
the same. Because when he came, he held her posses-
sively in place, his fingers making deep impressions in
her flesh. She burrowed her face in the hollow beneath
his shoulder and pinched the flesh there between her
teeth.

It was a long, slow, sweet climax. The aftermath was
as long, slow, and sweet.

Tiel was so totally relaxed, replete, that it felt as
though she had melted and become a part of him. She
couldn't distinguish her skin from his. She didn't want
to. She didn't even move when he pulled the sheet and
blanket up over them. She fell asleep there, with him still
sheathed in her softness, her ear resting on his heart.

"Tiel?"

"Hmm?"

"It's your alarm."

She muttered grumpily and pushed her hands deeper
into the warmth of his armpits.

"You've got to get up. The chopper's coming back for
you, remember?"

She did. But she didn't want to. She wanted to stay
exactly where she was for at least the next ten years. It
would take her that long to catch up on the sleep she
had lost last night. It would take her that long to get
enough of Doc.

"Come on. Up." He gave her fanny an affectionate smack. "Make yourself presentable before Sheriff Montez gets here."

Groaning, she rolled off him. Around a huge yawn, she asked, "How'd you know our arrangements?"

"He told me. That's how I knew where to find you." She gave him a misty look and he said, "Yes, he knew I wanted to know. Is that what you wanted to hear?"

"Yes."

"He and I are buddies. Play poker occasionally. He knows my story, why I moved out here, but he's good at keeping confidences."

"Even from the FBI."

"He asked if he could take my statement, and Calloway agreed. He had his hands full." He threw his legs over the side of the bed. "Mind if I use the bathroom first? I'll be quick."

"Be my guest."

In the process of bending down to pick up his boxers, he caught her with her hands far above her head, back arched, stretching lazily. He sat down on the edge of the bed, his eyes fixed on her breasts. He fondled the raised tip. "Maybe I don't want you to get in that chopper."

"Ask me not to and maybe I won't."

"You would."

"I have to," she said ruefully.

Sighing, he withdrew his hands. "Yeah." He got up and went into the bathroom.

"Maybe," Tiel whispered to herself, "I could convince you to come with me."

She removed a bra and panties set from her suitcase, put them on, and was just about to step into a pair of slacks when she sensed Doc watching her.

She turned, ready with a suggestive smile and a saucy

remark about peeping Toms. But his expression didn't invite either. In fact, he was practically bristling with rage.

Mystified, her lips parted to ask what the matter was when he held out his hand. Lying in his palm was the audio tape recorder. It had been in the pocket of her slacks, which she'd left along with her other dirty clothes in a pile on the commode lid. He'd moved them, found the recorder.

Her expression must have been a dead giveaway of her guilt because with a vicious punch of his thumb, he depressed the Play button and his voice cut across the silence. *"For instance, the hospital buckled beneath the weight of bad publicity. Bad publicity generated and nurtured by people like you."*

In a like manner, he stopped the tape and threw the recorder down onto the bed. "Take it." Looking scornfully at the tangled bed linens, he added, "You earned it."

"Doc, listen. I—"

"You got what you were after. A good story." Pushing her aside, he picked up his jeans and angrily thrust his legs into them.

"Will you stop with the righteous indignation and listen?"

He flung his hand toward the incriminating recorder. "I've heard enough. Did you get everything? All the juicy details of my personal life? I'm surprised you've tarried this long. I'd've thought you'd jog back to Dallas if necessary just so you could start assembling all the good material you've got on me."

He buttoned the fly of his jeans and yanked his shirt off the floor. "Oh, no, wait. You wanted to get fucked first. After Joe what's-his-name turned out to be a dud, your ego needed reinforcing."

The insult smarted and she reacted to it by striking back. "Who came to whose room? I didn't track you down. You came here, remember?"

He cursed when he couldn't find but one sock. He shoved his foot into his boot without it.

"Nor is it my fault that you're a good story," she shouted.

"I don't want to be a story. I never did."

"Too bad, Doc. You are. You simply are. Once notorious, you're now a hero. You saved lives last night. Do you think that'll go unnoticed? Those kids and their parents are going to talk about 'Doc.' So are the other hostages. Any reporter worth his paycheck is going to be clamoring for the lowdown. Even your friend Montez won't be able to shield you from the publicity. You would've made news no matter what. But since 'Doc' is the reclusive Dr. Bradley Stanwick, you're big news. Huge news."

He gestured toward the recorder again. "But you've got them all beat, don't you? Is there another recorder under the bed? Were you hoping to get titillating pillow talk?"

"Go to hell."

"I wouldn't put anything past you."

"I was doing my job."

"And here I thought I was speaking confidentially. But you're going to use it, aren't you? The stuff I thought I was confiding to you?"

"You're damn right I am!"

His jaw flexed with rage. He glared at her for several seconds, then marched toward the door. Tiel barged after him, grabbed his arm, and pulled him around. "It could be the best thing that ever happened to you."

He yanked his arm free of her grasp. "I fail to see that."

"It could force you to face up to the fact that you were wrong to run away. Last...last night," she said, stuttering in her haste to make her point before he stormed out. "You told Ronnie that he couldn't run away from his problems. That running from them was no solution. But isn't that exactly what you did?

"You moved out here and buried your head in this West Texas sand, refusing to accept what you know to be true. That you're a gifted healer. That you could make a difference. That you *were* making a difference. For patients and families facing a death sentence, you were granting reprieves. God knows what you could do in the future.

"But because of your pride, and anger, and disillusionment with your colleagues, you abandoned it. You threw out the baby with the bathwater. If this story draws you back into the limelight, if there's a chance it will motivate you to return to your practice, then I'll be damned before I'll apologize for it."

He turned his back on her and opened the door.

"Doc?" she cried.

But all he said was, "Your ride is here."

Chapter 17

———❖———

Tiel's cubicle in the newsroom was a disaster area. It usually was, but more so now than usual. She had received hundreds of notes, cards, and letters from colleagues and viewers, complimenting her excellent coverage of the Davison-Dendy story and commending her for the heroic role she'd played in it. Many were yet to be opened. They had been piled into wobbly, uneven stacks.

There weren't enough surfaces to accommodate the number of floral arrangements delivered over the past week, so she had distributed them to offices and conference areas throughout the building.

Vern and Gladys had sent her a mail-order cheesecake that would have fed five thousand. The newsroom staff had gorged themselves, and there was still more than half left.

As anticipated, she had been the center of attention, and not only on a local level. She had been interviewed by reporters from global news operations, including

CNN and Bloomberg. Because of the compelling human element, the love story, the emergency birth of the baby, and the dramatic denouement, the story had piqued the interest of TV audiences all over the world.

She'd been asked by a local car dealership to do their commercials, an offer she declined. National women's magazines were proposing feature articles on everything from her secrets of success to the decor of her house. She was the undeclared Woman of the Week.

And she had never been more miserable.

She was making a futile stab at clearing off her desk when Gully joined her. "Hey, kid."

"I took the rest of the cheesecake to the cafeteria and left it there on a first come, first served basis."

"I got the last piece."

"Your arteries will never forgive me."

"Have I told you what a great job you did?"

"It's always nice to hear."

"Great job."

"Thanks. But it's left me drained. I'm tired."

"You look it. In fact you look like hammered shit." She tossed him a dirty glance over her shoulder. "Just calling it like I see it."

"Didn't your mother ever tell you that some things are better left unsaid?"

"What's the matter with you?"

"I told you, Gully, I'm—"

"You're not just tired. I know tired, and this isn't tired. You should be lit up like a Christmas tree. You're not your normal, hyperactive, supercharged self. Is it Linda Harper? Are you sulking because she got the jump on you and stole some of your thunder?"

"No." She methodically ripped open another envelope and read the congratulatory note inside. *I love your reports on the TV. You're my roll* [sic] *model. I want to be just like you when I grow up. I like your hair too.*

Gully said, "I can't believe you didn't recognize the Doc of standoff fame as Dr. Bradley Stanwick."

"Hmm."

Gully continued, undaunted in spite of her seeming disinterest. "Let me put it another way. I *don't* believe you didn't recognize him as Dr. Bradley Stanwick."

The change in Gully's tone of voice was unmistakable, and there was no way to avoid addressing it. She laid down the note from the girl who identified herself as Kimberly, a fifth-grader, and slowly swiveled her chair around to face Gully.

He looked down at her for a long moment. Her eyes never wavered. Neither said anything.

Finally, he dragged his hand down his face, the sagging skin stretching like a rubber Halloween mask. "I suppose you had your reasons for protecting his identity."

"He asked me not to."

"Oh." He slapped his forehead with his palm. "Of course! What's wrong with me? The subject of the story said, 'I don't want to be on TV,' so, naturally, you omitted an important element of the story."

"It didn't cost your news operation anything, Gully." Her mood testy, she stood up and began tossing personal items into her bag in preparation of leaving. "Linda got it. So what are you complaining about?"

"Was I complaining? Did you hear me complaining?"

"It sounded like complaining."

"I'm just curious as to why my ace reporter wimped out on me."

"I didn't—"

"You wimped! Big-time. I want to know why."

She spun around to confront him. "Because it got..." She stopped shouting, drew herself up, took a deep breath, and ended on a much softer note. "Complicated."

"Complicated."

"Complicated." She reached around him for her suit jacket, lifted it off the wall hook, and pulled it on, avoiding his incisive eyes. "It's sort of like Deep Throat."

"It's nothing like Deep Throat, who was a source. Bradley Stanwick was an active player. Subject matter. Fair game."

"That's a distinction we should debate sometime. Some other time. When I'm not about to leave for vacation."

"So you're still going?" He fell into step behind her as she left the cubicle and began wending her way through the newsroom toward the rear of the building.

"I need the time away more than ever. You approved my request for days off."

"I know," he said querulously. "But I've had second thoughts. You know what I was thinking? I was thinking that you should produce a pilot *Nine Live* show. This cancer-doctor-cum-cowboy would be a dynamite first guest. Get him to talk about the investigation into his wife's death. What's his viewpoint on euthanasia? Did he euthanize her?"

"He was motivated to, but he didn't."

"See? We've got a provocative dialogue going already. You could segue into his participation in the standoff. It'd be great! We could show this pilot show to the suits upstairs. Maybe air it as a special report one night following the news. It'd be your ticket to the *Nine Live* hostess spot."

"Don't hold your breath, Gully." She pushed open the heavy exit door leading to the employee parking lot. The pavement was as hot as a griddle.

"How come?" He followed her out. "This is what you've wanted, Tiel. What you've worked for. You'd better grab it, or it could still be snatched away from you. They could give the show to Linda, especially if they ever find out you knew about Stanwick all along. Postpone this trip until this is settled."

"And then I won't be able to leave because of all the production meetings." She shook her head. "Uh-uh, Gully. I'm going."

"I don't get you. Is it PMS, or what?"

Refusing to take umbrage, she smiled. "I'm tired of the dance, Gully. I'm weary of the constant jockeying for position, and the paranoia it breeds. Management knows what I can do. They're aware of my popularity with viewers, and it's higher now than it's ever been. They've got years of my work, ratings, and awards to remind them that I'm the best choice for that job."

She opened her car door and tossed her bag inside. "They'll be hearing from my agent while I'm away. I'm making *Nine Live* a condition of my contract. I don't get the show, they don't get a renewal. And I've received at least a hundred other offers this week to back up that mandate."

She leaned forward and kissed his cheek, which had gone flabby with astonishment. "I love you, Gully. I love my work. But it's *work*; it's no longer my life."

She made one stop on her way out of town—at a Dumpster behind a supermarket. She tossed two things into it. One was an audiocassette recording. The other was the two-hour videotape from Gladys and Vern's camcorder.

———◆———

Tiel cursed the hopelessly snarled fishing line. "Dammit!"

"They aren't biting?"

Thinking she was alone, she jumped, executing a quick turn at the same time. Her knees went weak at the sight of him. He was leaning negligently against a tree trunk, his tall, lean form and cowboy garb in harmony with the rugged landscape.

"I didn't know you could fish," he remarked.

He'd come all this way to talk about fishing? Okay. "Obviously I can't." She held out the tangled line and frowned. "But since that's what one is supposed to do when there's a clear mountain stream running behind one's vacation condo... Doc, what are you doing here?"

"Good news about Ronnie, huh?"

Ronnie Davison had been upgraded from critical to good condition. If he continued to improve, he would be released to return home within a few days. "Very good news. About Sabra too. She's already back in Fort Worth. I talked to her last night by phone. She and her mother are going to rear Katherine. Ronnie will have unlimited visitation, but they've decided to postpone getting married for a couple of years. Regardless of the outcome of his legal entanglements, they've agreed to wait and see if the relationship can stand the test of time."

"Smart kids. If it's right, it'll happen."

"That's their thinking."

"Well, Dendy can be glad he won't be charged with murder."

"No, but dozens of witnesses saw him attempt it. I hope they throw the book at him."

"I second that motion. He nearly cost several lives."

The conversation flagged after that. The silence was filled by the chirping of birds and the incessant, friendly gurgle of the stream. When the pressure inside Tiel's chest reached the cracking point, she asked again, "What are you doing here?"

"I got a cheesecake from Vern and Gladys."

"So did I."

"Huge."

"Humongous."

Feeling silly holding the casting rod, she laid it at her feet, but immediately wished she hadn't. Now she had nothing to do with her hands, which suddenly seemed excessively large and conspicuous. She slid them into the rear pockets of her jeans, palms out. "It's a beautiful place, isn't it?"

"Sure is."

"When did you arrive?"

"About an hour ago."

"Oh."

Then, miserably, "Doc, what are you doing here?"

"I came to thank you."

She lowered her head and looked down at her feet. Her sneakers had sunk sole-deep into the mud of the creek bed. "Don't. Thank me, I mean. I couldn't use the recording. I had a video, too. From Gladys's camcorder. The quality of the tape wasn't very good, but no other reporter in the world had it."

She took a deep breath, glanced up at him, then back down. "But you were on the tape. Recognizable. And I didn't want to exploit you after... after what happened in the motel. It was personal then. I couldn't exploit you without exploiting part of myself too. So I threw them away. No one ever saw or heard them."

"Hmm. Well, that's not what I was thanking you for."

Her head sprang up. "Huh?"

"I saw your stories about the standoff, and they were great. I mean that. Outstanding broadcast journalism. You deserve all the accolades you received. And I appreciate your keeping our private conversations private. You were right about the exposure. It was bound to happen with or without help from you. I see that now."

For once in her life, she had nothing to say.

"The reason I came to thank you is for making me take a hard look at myself. My life. How wasteful it's been. After Shari died and all that followed, I needed solitude, time and space to think things through, reassess. That used up…say six months. The rest of the time I've been doing exactly what you said, hiding. Punishing myself. Taking the coward's way out."

The pressure building inside her now wasn't tension, it was emotion. Maybe love. Okay, love. She wanted to go to him, hold him, but she wanted to hear what he had to say. Furthermore, he needed to say it.

"I'm going back. I spent the past week in Dallas talking to some doctors and researchers, newcomers who share my aggressive approach to fighting this thing, doctors who are tired of having to go through umpteen committees and legal counsels to get approval of a new treatment when the patient is suffering and all other options have been exhausted. We'd like to take medicine out of the hands of lawyers and bureaucrats and return it to the doctors. So, we're forming a group, pooling our resources and specialities—" He looked hard at her. "Are you crying?"

"The sun's in my eyes."

"Oh. Well. That's what I came to tell you."

Economically, efficiently, in as business-like a manner as she could, she rubbed the tears from her eyes. "You didn't have to travel all this way. You could have e-mailed me, or called."

"That would have been cowardly too. I needed to say this in person, face-to-face."

"How'd you know where to find me?"

"I went to the TV station. Talked to Gully, who also asked me to deliver a message." A small bob of her head indicated that she was listening. "He said, 'Tell her I ain't dense. I just figured out the meaning of complicated.' Does that make sense?"

She laughed. "Yes."

"Care to explain?"

"Maybe later. If you're staying."

"If you don't mind my company."

"I think I can tolerate it."

He returned her wide smile, but his faltered, and his expression turned serious again. "We're both pretty intense when it comes to our work, Tiel."

"Which I believe is part of the attraction."

"It won't be easy."

"Nothing worthwhile is."

"We don't know where it will lead."

"But we know where we hope it will. We also know it will lead to nowhere if we don't give it a try."

"I loved my wife, Tiel, and love can hurt."

"Not being loved hurts worse. Maybe we can find a way to love each other without it hurting."

"God, I want to touch you."

"Doc," she murmured. Then she laughed. "Bradley? Brad? How do I call you?"

"A simple 'Come here' will do for now."

Then he closed the distance separating them.

About the Author

Sandra Brown is the author of sixty-eight *New York Times* bestsellers. There are more than eighty million copies of her books in print worldwide, and her work has been translated into thirty-four languages. In 2008, the International Thriller Writers Association named Brown its Thriller Master, the organization's highest honor. She has served as president of Mystery Writers of America and holds an honorary doctorate of humane letters from Texas Christian University. She lives in Texas.

For more information you can visit:
   SandraBrown.net
   Facebook.com/AuthorSandraBrown
   @Sandra_BrownNYT

A rising star TV journalist determined to get the exclusive of her lifetime—by any means necessary.

An infuriating private investigator who wants her out of his family's life—but finds her impossible to resist.

A catastrophic interview that puts them both in mortal danger.

#1 *New York Times* bestselling author Sandra Brown delivers relentless suspense, staggering twists, and heart-pounding romance in her tantalizing new thriller.

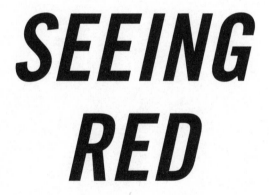

SEEING RED

PLEASE TURN THE PAGE FOR A PREVIEW.

ON SALE AUGUST 2017

Prologue

———◈———

Did you think you were going to die?"

The Major pursed his lips with disapproval. "That question wasn't on the list I approved."

"Which is why I didn't ask it while the cameras were rolling. But there's no one here now but us. I'm asking off the record. Were you in fear of your life? Did dying cross your mind?"

"I didn't stop to think about it."

Kerra Bailey tilted her head and regarded him with doubt. "That sounds like a canned answer."

The seventy-year-old gave her the smile that had won him the heart of a nation. "It is."

"All right," she said. "I'll respectfully and graciously withdraw the question."

She could pass on it because, after all, she'd got what she'd come for: the first interview of any kind that he had granted in more than three years. In the days leading up to this evening's live telecast from his home, he and she had become well acquainted.

They'd engaged in some lively discussions, often taking opposing views.

Kerra looked up at the stag head mounted above his mantel. "I stand by my aversion to having the eyes of dead animals staring down at me."

He chuckled. "Venison is food. And keeping the herd thinned out is ecologically—"

"I've heard all the justifications from other hunters. I just don't understand how anyone could place a beautiful animal like that in the crosshairs and pull the trigger."

"Neither of us is going to win this argument," he said, to which she replied with matching stubbornness, "Neither of us is going to concede it, either."

He blurted a short laugh that ended in a dry cough. "You're right." He glanced over at the tall gun cabinet in the corner of the vast room, then pushed himself out of his brown leather La-Z-Boy, walked over to the cabinet, and opened the paned-glass front.

He removed one of the rifles. "I took that particular deer with this rifle. It was my wife's last Christmas present to me." He ran his hand along the bluish barrel. "I haven't used it since she died."

Kerra was touched to see this softer side of him. "I wish she could have been here for the interview."

"So do I. I miss her every day."

"What was it like for her, being married to America's hero?"

"Oh, she was super-impressed," he said around a chuckle as he propped the rifle in the corner between the cabinet and the wall. "She nagged me only every other day about leaving my dirty socks on the floor rather than putting them in the hamper."

Kerra laughed, but her thoughts turned to the Major's son and his aversion to his father's fame. She had felt obligated to invite him to appear on the program, perhaps in the final segment. Using explicit language that left no room for misinterpretation, he had declined. *Thank God.*

The Major crossed to the built-in bar. "So much talking has made me thirsty. I could use a drink. What would you like?"

"Nothing for me." She stood and retrieved her bag from where she'd set it on the floor beside her chair. "As soon as the crew gets back, we need to hit the road."

The Major had had a local restaurant prepare and deliver a cold fried chicken picnic supper for her and the five-person production crew. After they'd eaten, packing up the gear had taken an hour, but when all was done, Kerra had asked the others to go gas up the van for their two-hour drive back to Dallas, while she stayed behind. She had wanted a few minutes alone with the Major in order to thank him properly.

She began, "Major, I must tell you—"

He turned to her and interrupted. "You've said it, Kerra. Repeatedly. You don't need to say it again."

"You may not need to hear it again, but I need to say it." Her voice turned husky with emotion. "Please accept my heartfelt thank you for...well, for everything. I can't adequately express my gratitude. It knows no bounds."

Matching her solemn tone, he replied, "You're welcome."

She smiled at him and took a short breath. "May I call you every once in a while? Come visit if I'm ever out this way again?"

"I'd like that very much."

They shared a long look, leaving the many insufficient words unspoken, but conveying to each other a depth of feeling. Then, to break the sentimental mood, he rubbed his hands together. "Sure you won't have a drink?"

"No, but I would take advantage of your bathroom." She left her coat in the chair but shouldered her bag.

"You know where it is."

This making the fourth time she'd been to his house, she was familiar with the layout. The living area looked like a miniature Texas museum, with cowhide rugs on the distressed hardwood floor, Remington reproductions in bronze of cowboys in action, and pieces of furniture that made the Major's recliner seem small by comparison.

One of the offshoots of the main room was a hallway, and the first door to the left was the powder room, although that feminine-sounding name was incongruous with the hand soap dispenser in the shape of a longhorn steer.

She was drying her hands at the sink and checking her reflection in the framed mirror above it, making a mental note to call her hairdresser—maybe a few more highlights around her face?—when the door latch rattled, calling her attention to it. "Major? Is the crew back? I'll be right out."

He didn't respond, although she sensed someone on the other side of the door.

She replaced the hand towel in the iron ring mounted on the wall beside the sink and was reaching for her shoulder bag when she heard the *bang*.

Her mind instantly clicked back to the Major. Taking the rifle from the cabinet. Not replacing it in the rack. If he'd been doing so now and it had accidentally discharged... *Oh my God!*

She lunged for the door and grabbed hold of the knob, but snatched her hand back when she heard a voice, not the Major's, say, "How do you like being dead so far?"

Kerra clapped her hand over her mouth to hold back a wail of disbelief and horror. She heard footsteps thudding around in the living room. One set? Two? It was hard to tell, and fear had robbed her of mental acuity. She did, however, have the presence of mind to switch off the bathroom light.

Holding her breath, she listened, tracking the footsteps as they crossed rugs, struck hardwood, and then, to her mounting horror, entered the hallway. They came even with the bathroom door and stopped.

Moving as soundlessly as possible, she backed away from the door, feeling her way past the sink and toilet in the darkness, until she came up against the bead-board wall. She tried to keep her breathing silent, though her lips moved around a prayer of only one repeated word: Please, please, please.

Whoever was on the other side of the door tried turning the knob and found it locked. It was tried a second time, then the door shook as an attempt was made to force it open. To whoever was trying to open it, the locked door could only mean one thing: someone was on the other side.

She'd been discovered.

Another set of footsteps came rushing from the living area. The door was battered against with what she imagined was the stock of a rifle.

She had nothing with which to defend herself against armed assailants. If they had in fact murdered the Major, and if they got past that door, she would die, too.

Escape was her only option and it had to be now.

The double-hung window behind her was small, but it was the only chance she had of getting out alive. She felt for the lock holding the sashes together, twisted it open, then placed her fingers in the depressions of the lower sash and pulled up with all her might. It didn't budge.

Several blasts sounded in rapid succession, shooting at the lock.

Because silence was no longer necessary, Kerra was sobbing now, taking in noisy gulps of air. Please, please, please. She whimpered the entreaty for salvation from a source stronger than her because she felt powerless.

She put all she had into raising the window, and it became unstuck with such suddenness that it took her aback for perhaps one heartbeat. Another shot was fired and the bullet struck the porcelain sink and ricocheted into the wall.

She threw one leg over the windowsill and bent practically in half in order to get her head and shoulders through. When they cleared the opening, she launched herself out and dropped to the ground.

She landed on her shoulder. A spike of pain took her breath. Her left arm went numb and useless. She rolled onto her stomach and pushed herself up with her right arm. After taking a few staggering steps to regain her balance, she took off in a sprint. Behind her she heard the bathroom door crashing open.

A blast from a shotgun deafened her and sheared off the branch of a young mesquite tree. She kept running. It fired again, striking a boulder and creating shrapnel that struck her legs like darts.

How many misses would they get before hitting her?

There were no city lights, only a sliver of moon. The darkness made her a more difficult target, but it also prevented her from seeing more than a few feet ahead of her. She ran blindly, stumbling over rocks, scrub brush, and uneven ground.

Please, please, please.

Then without warning, the earth gave out beneath her. She pitched forward, grabbing hold of nothing but air. She was helpless to catch herself before smashing into the ground and rolling, sliding, falling.

Chapter 1

———◆———

Six days earlier

Trapper was in a virtual coma when the knocking started.

"Bloody hell," he mumbled into the throw pillow beneath his head. His face would bear the imprint of the upholstery when he got up. *If* he ever got up. Right now he had no intention of moving, not even to open his eyes.

The knocking might have been part of a dream. Maybe a construction worker somewhere in the building was tapping the walls in search of studs. An urban woodpecker? Whatever. If he ignored the noise, maybe it would go away.

But after fifteen seconds of blessed silence, there came another knock-knock. Trapper croaked, "I'm closed. Come back later."

The next three knocks were insistent.

Swearing, he rolled onto his back, sailed the drool-damp pillow across the office, and laid his forearm over his eyes to block the daylight. The window blinds were only partially open, but those cheerful, skinny strips of sunshine made his eyeballs throb.

Keeping one eye closed, he eased his feet off the sofa and onto the floor. When he stood, he stumbled over his discarded boots. His big toe sent his cell phone sliding across the floor and underneath a chair. If he were to bend down that far, he doubted his ability to return upright, so he left his phone where it was.

It wasn't like it rang all that often anyway.

Holding the heel of his hand against his pounding temple, and with one eye remaining closed, he managed to reach the other side of his office without bumping into the bottom drawer of the metal file cabinet. For no reason he could remember, it was standing open.

Through the frosted glass upper half of the door he made out a form just as it raised its fist to knock again. To prevent the further agony that would induce, Trapper flipped the lock and opened the door a crack.

He sized her up within two seconds. "You've got the wrong office. One flight up. First door to the left off the elevator."

He was about to shut the door when she said, "John Trapper?"

Shit. Had he forgotten an appointment? He scratched the top of his head, where his hair hurt down to the follicles. "What time is it?"

"Twelve fifteen."

"What day?"

She took a breath and let it out slowly. "Monday."

He looked her up and down and came back to her face. "Who are you?"

"Kerra Bailey."

The name didn't ring any bells, but it would be hard

to hear them over the jackhammer inside his skull. "Look, if it's about the parking meter—"

"The one in front of the building? The one that's been flattened?"

"I'll pay to have it replaced. I'll cover any other damages. I would have left a note to that effect, but I didn't have anything on me to write—"

"I'm not here about the parking meter."

"Oh. Hmm. Did we have an appointment?"

"No."

"Well, now's not a good time for me, Ms...." He went blank.

"Bailey," she said, in the same impatient tone in which she'd said *Monday*.

"Right. Call me, and we'll schedule—"

"It's important that I talk to you sooner rather than later. May I come in?" She gestured at the door, which Trapper had kept open only a few inches.

A woman who looked like her, he hated turning down for anything. But, hell. His head felt as dense as a bowling ball. His shirt was unbuttoned, the tail hanging loose. He hoped his fly was zipped, but in case it wasn't, he didn't risk calling attention to it by checking. His breath would stop a clock.

He glanced behind him at the disarray: suit jacket and tie slung over the back of a chair; boots in front of the sofa, one upright, the other lying on its side; one black sock draped over the armrest, the other sock God-only-knew-where; an empty bottle of Dom precariously close to rolling off the corner of his desk.

He needed a shower. He really needed to pee.

But he also really *really* needed clients, and she had "money" written all over her. Her handbag, literally so. It was the size of a small suitcase and covered in designer initials. Even if she had been looking for the tax attorney on the next floor up, she would have been slumming.

Besides, when had he ever been known to say no to a lady in distress?

He stepped back and opened the door, motioning her toward the two straight chairs facing his desk. He kicked the file cabinet drawer shut with his heel and still got to his desk ahead of her in time to relocate an empty but smelly Chinese food carton and the latest issue of *Maxim*. He'd ranked the cover shot among his top ten faves, but she might take exception to that much areolae.

She sat in one chair and placed her bag in the other. As he rounded the desk, he buttoned the middle button of his shirt and ran a hand across his mouth and chin to check for remaining drool.

As he dropped into his desk chair, he caught her looking at the gravity-defying champagne bottle. He rescued it from the corner of the desk and set it gently in the trash can to avoid a clatter. "Buddy of mine got married."

"Last night?"

"Saturday afternoon."

Her eyebrow arched. "It must have been some wedding."

He shrugged, then leaned back in his chair. "Who recommended me?"

"No one. I got the address off your website."

Trapper had forgotten he even had one. He'd paid a college kid seventy-five bucks to do whatever it was you do to get a website up. That was the last he'd thought of it. This was the first client it had yielded.

She looked like she could afford much better.

"I apologize for showing up without an appointment," she said. "I tried calling you several times this morning, but kept getting your voice mail."

Trapper shot a look toward the chair his phone had slid underneath. "I silenced my phone for the wedding. Guess I forgot to turn it back on." As discreetly as possible, he shifted in his chair in a vain attempt to give his bladder some breathing room.

"Well, it's sooner rather than later, Ms. Bailey. You said it was important, but not important enough for you to make an appointment. What can I do for you?"

"I'd like for you to intervene on my behalf and convince your father to grant me an interview."

He looked at her, thinking that she appeared to be sane. He would have said *Come again?* or *Pardon?* or *I didn't quite catch that*, but she had articulated perfectly, so what he said was, "Is this a fucking joke?"

"No."

"Seriously, who put you up to this?"

"No one, Mr. Trapper."

"Just plain Trapper is fine, but it doesn't matter what you call me because we don't have anything else to say to each other." He stood up and headed for the door.

"You haven't even heard me out."

"Yeah. I have. Now if you'll excuse me, I gotta take a piss and then I've got a hangover to sleep off. Close the door on your way out. This neighborhood, I hope your car's still there when you get back to it."

He stalked out in bare feet and went down the drab hallway to the men's room. He used the urinal, then went over to the sink and looked at himself in the cloudy, cracked mirror above it. A pile of dog shit had nothing on him.

He bent down and scooped tap water into his mouth

until his thirst was no longer raging, then ducked his head under the faucet. He shook water from his hair and dried his face with paper towels. With one more nod toward respectability, he buttoned his shirt as he was walking back to his office.

She was still there. Which didn't come as that much of a surprise. She looked the type that didn't give up easily.

Before he could order her out, she said, "Why would you object to the Major giving an interview?"

"I wouldn't. I don't give a crap. But he won't do it, and I think you already know that or you wouldn't have come to me, because I'm the last person on the planet who could convince him to do anything."

"Why is that?"

He recognized that cleverly laid trap for what it was, and didn't step into it. "Let me guess, Ms. Bailey. I'm your last resort?" Her expression was as good as an admission. "Before coming to me, how many times did you ask the Major yourself?"

"I've called him thirteen times."

"How many times did he hang up on you?"

"Thirteen."

"Rude bastard."

Under her breath, she said, "It must be a family trait."

Trapper only smiled. "It's the only one he and I have in common." He studied her for a moment. "You get points for tenacity. Most give up long before thirteen attempts. Who do you work for?"

"A network O and O—owned and operated—in Dallas."

"You're on TV? In Dallas?"

"I do feature stories. Human interest, things like that.

Occasionally one makes it to the network's Sunday evening news show."

Trapper was familiar with the program but he didn't remember ever having watched it.

He knew for certain that he'd never seen her, not even on the local station, or he would've remembered. She had straight, sleek light brown hair with blonder streaks close to her face. Brown eyes as large as a doe's. One inch below the outside corner of the left one was a beauty mark the same dark chocolate color as her irises. Her complexion was creamy, her lips plump and pink, and he was reluctant to pull his gaze away from them.

But he did. "Sorry, but you drove over here for nothing."

"Mr. Trapper—"

"You're wasting your time. The Major retired from public life years ago."

"Three to be exact. And he didn't merely retire. He went into seclusion. Why do you think he did that?"

"My guess is that he got sick of talking about it."

"What about you?"

"I was sick of it long before that."

"How old were you?"

"At the time of the bombing? Eleven. Fifth grade."

"Your father's sudden celebrity must have affected you."

"Not really."

She watched him for a moment, then said softly, "That's impossible. It had to have impacted your life as dramatically as it did his."

He squinted one eye. "You know what this sounds like? Leading questions, like you're trying to interview *me*. In which case, you're S.O.L. because I'm not going to talk about the Major, or me, or effects on my life. Ever. Not to anybody."

She reached into the oversized bag and took out an 8x10 reproduction of a photograph, then laid it on the desk and pushed it toward him.

Without even glancing down at it, he pushed it back. "I've seen it." For the second time, he stood up, went to the door and opened it, then stood there, hands on hips, waiting.

She hesitated, then sighed with resignation, hiked the strap of her bag onto her shoulder, and joined him at the door. "I caught you at a bad time."

"No, this is about as good as I get."

"Would you consider meeting me later, after you've had time to..." She made a gesture that encompassed his sorry state. "To feel better? I could outline what I want to do. We could talk about it over dinner."

"Nothing to talk about."

"I'm paying."

He shook his head. "Thanks anyway."

She gnawed the inside of her cheek as though trying to determine which tactic to use to try to persuade him. Regarding that, he could offer some salacious suggestions, but she probably wouldn't go that far, and even if she did, afterward he'd still say no to her request.

She took a look around the office before coming back to him. With the tip of her index finger, she underlined the words stenciled on the frosted glass of the door. "Private Investigator."

"So it says."

"Your profession is to investigate things, solve mysteries."

He snuffled. That was his former profession. Nowadays he was retained by tearful wives wanting him to confirm that their husbands were screwing around. If he managed to get pictures, it doubled his fee. Distraught parents paid him to track down runaway teens, whom he usually found exchanging alleyway blow jobs for heroin.

He wouldn't call the work he was doing mystery-solving. Or investigation, for that matter.

But to her, he said, "Yeah. I'm a regular Sherlock Holmes."

"Are you licensed?"

"Oh, yeah. I have a gun, bullets, everything."

"Do you have a magnifying glass?"

The question took him aback only because she hadn't asked it in jest. She was serious. "What for?" he asked.

Those pouty lips fashioned an enigmatic smile and she whispered, "Figure it out."

Keeping her eyes on his, she reached into an inside pocket of her bag and withdrew a business card. She didn't hand it to him, but stuck it in a crack between the frosted glass pane and the door frame, adjacent to the words that spelled out his job description.

"When you change your mind, my cell number is on the card."

———— ◦ ————

Hell would freeze over first.

Trapper slammed the office door behind her, plucked the business card from the slit, and flipped it straight into the trash can.

Eager to go home and sleep off the remainder of his hangover in a more comfortable surrounding, he snatched up the sock on the armrest of the sofa and went in search of the other.

After several frustrating minutes and a litany of elaborate profanity, he found it inside one of his boots. He pulled on his socks, but decided he needed an aspirin before he finished dressing. Padding over to his desk, he opened the lap drawer in the hope of discovering a forgotten bottle of analgesics.

That damned photograph was there in plain sight where he couldn't miss it.

But whether looking at it, or acknowledging it in any manner, or even denying its existence, he was never truly free of it. He had lied to Kerra Bailey. His life was never the same after that photograph went global twenty-five years ago.

Trapper plopped down into his desk chair and looked at the cursed thing. His head hurt, his eyes were scratchy, his throat and mouth were still parched. But even realizing that it was masochistic, he reached across the desk and slid the photo closer to him.

Everyone in the entire world had seen it at least once over the past quarter century. Among prize-winning, defining-moment, editorial photographs, it ranked right up there with the raising of the flag on Iwo Jima, the sailor kissing the nurse in Times Square on V-E Day, the naked Vietnamese girl running from napalm, the twin towers of the World Trade Center aflame and crumbling.

But before 9/11, there was the Pegasus Hotel bombing in downtown Dallas. It had rocked a city still trying to live down the Kennedy assassination, had destroyed a landmark building, had snuffed out the lives of one hundred ninety-seven people. Half that number had been critically injured.

Major Franklin Trapper had led a handful of struggling survivors out of the smoldering rubble to safety.

A photographer who worked for one of Dallas's newspapers had been eating lunch at his desk in the city room when the first bomb detonated. The blast deafened him. The repercussion shook his building and created cracks in the aggregate floor beneath his desk. Windows shattered.

But like an old fire horse, he was conditioned to run toward a disaster. He snatched up his camera, bolted down three flights of fire stairs, and, upon exiting the newspaper building, dashed toward the source of the black plume of smoke that had already engulfed the skyline.

He reached the scene of terror and chaos ahead of emergency responders who would soon be scrambling to evacuate the area for blocks around and to set up street blockades to keep out anyone who wasn't search-and-rescue or medical personnel.

The photographer began snapping pictures, including the one that became iconic: Franklin Trapper, recently retired from the U.S. Army, emerging from the smoking building leading a pathetic group of dazed, scorched, bleeding, choking people, one child cradled in his arms, a woman holding on to his coattail, a man whose tibia had a compound fracture using him as a crutch.

The photographer, now deceased, had won a Pulitzer for his picture. The act of heroism he had captured on film during his lunch hour immediately earned him and the photo immortality.

And, as Trapper well knew, immortality lasted for fucking ever.

The story behind the photograph and the people in it wouldn't come to light until later, when those who were hospitalized were able to relate their individual accounts.

Though, by the time the tales were told, the Trappers' front yard in suburban Dallas had become an encampment for media. The Major—as he came to be known—had been ordained a national symbol of bravery and self-sacrifice.

For years following that day in 1992, he was a sought-after public speaker. He was given every honor and award there was to be bestowed, and many were initiated and named for him. He was invited to the White House by every subsequent administration. At state dinners he was introduced to visiting foreign dignitaries who paid homage to his courage.

Over time, new disasters produced new heroes. The fireman carrying the toddler from the Oklahoma City bombing overshadowed the Major's celebrity for a time, but soon he was back on TV talk show guest lists and the after-dinner speaker circuit.

Then three years ago, it came to a screeching halt.

He now lived very privately, avoiding the limelight and refusing requests for public appearances and interviews.

But his legend lived on. Which was why journalists, biographers, and movie producers emerged now and again, seeking time with him to make their particular pitch. He never granted them that time.

Until today none had ever sought out Trapper's help to gain access to the Major.

Kerra Bailey's audacity was galling enough. But damn her for snagging his interest with that remark about the magnifying glass. What could he possibly see in that photograph that he hadn't seen ten thousand times?

He longed for a hot shower, an aspirin, his bed and soft pillow.

"Fuck it." He opened his desk's lap drawer and, instead of reaching for the bottle of Bayer, searched all the way to the back of it and came up with the long-forgotten magnifying glass.

Four hours later, he was still in his desk chair, still reeking, head still aching, eyes still scratchy. But everything else had changed.

He set down the magnifier, pushed the fingers of both hands up through his hair, and held his head between his palms. "Son of a bitch."